AKA DOCTOR

MANDATORY/MINIMUM

8-31-04

CATHY

TO DREAM THE DREAM.

ALWAYS

STEVE

AKA DOCTOR

Copyright © 2004 by Steven Maros

ISBN 0-7414-2187-9

Published by:

INFI∞ITY
PUBLISHING.COM

1094 New Dehaven Street, Suite 100
West Conshohocken, PA 19428-2713
Info@buybooksontheweb.com
www.buybooksontheweb.com
Toll-free (877) BUY BOOK
Local Phone (610) 941-9999
Fax (610) 941-9959

Printed in the United States of America

Printed on Recycled Paper

Published August 2004

DEDICATED

To my friend, my wife, Laurie

CONTENTS

DOWNSIDE

Trying to keep a positive attitude while you are handcuffed is hard to do. I did my best. My mind wandered off to when I lived in St. Petersburg, Florida. The year was nineteen seventy-seven. Today was March of nineteen ninety-two. I learned to sail in St. Petersburg. Today I was forty years old. My six foot, two inch frame was strong, my brown hair, was still sort of brown. I looked up into the blue sky. I could have sworn my brown eyes turned blue.

My friend Paul was sitting next to me in the cockpit of his thirty six foot sailing vessel, Driven. Paul was a little shorter than me. He had black hair, brown eyes. Paul had a rugged look to him, yet he was an artist. We met while driving taxi in L.A. Paul was also handcuffed. The time was just before seven in the morning. The sky was clear. The wind was from the northwest at twelve knots. This would have been a perfect sailing day along the middle Baja, Mexican coast. Paul and I were heading home to Long Beach, California. Paul grew up in Long Beach. I had just moved to Long Beach for south of the border business reasons. Today was the downside to this business.

We had sailed to Acapulco earlier that year. We both loved the art of sailing. Sailing came naturally to us in our lives. The reality of this day was. A three man Coast Guard boarding party was onboard. They motored their small inflatable boat over to us to do an Initial Safety Inspection (ISI). They motored over to us from the six hundred foot, U.S. Guided Missile Cruiser they were onboard. The Cruiser houses three hundred and fifty people. They boarded us two hundred fifty miles south of San Diego. They did this boarding at three in the morning. We thought how nice it was for them to care about our safety, at that hour of the morning.

1

Paul and I looked at each other with questions in our eyes. How the hell did this happen? Why did it take so long to do the inspection? It took three hours and forty-one minutes to find the hidden compartments. How did they find us out here in the middle of the Mexican Coast?

We found the answers to these questions weeks later. The sailing vessel Driven was towed for two days into San Diego. Paul and myself were taken prisoner onboard the Guided Missile Cruiser. We were placed into the hands of U.S. Customs agents at the Naval Shipyard, Long Beach, California. From the shipyard we were taken to Metropolitan Detention Center, located in downtown L.A. where we were booked.

DECLARATION

The United States District Court, for the Central District of California was located across from the detention center, on Spring Street. Paul and I were placed into a car with two U.S. Customs agents. We were brought to a large holding cell located in the bottom of the courthouse. Four hours later, about ten in the morning, two Marshals escorted us to a courtroom on the second floor. Paul was appointed an attorney. Tony was Paul's attorneys name. My appointed attorney for the hearing was named Reed.

Our attorney's advised us of what was going on in the courtroom today. I recognized the Coast Guard Boatswain's, Huey, Dewey and Louie sitting in the courtroom. They were wearing white uniforms, just like Richard Gere wore in the movie Officer and a Gentleman. I smiled back at them.

My attorney told me a little of his background. I liked the guy. He was slender, wore black-rimmed glasses, black hair, brown eyes. He had a nice personality, but nevertheless he was still an attorney. We seemed to be the same age. I would soon be forty-one. If I get the Mandatory/Minimum sentence of ten years, I will be forty-nine when I get out.

Paul's attorney had a reputation as a heavy hitter. He had rumors of Mafia connections, and all that happy kind of stuff. He even looked the part. Paul is Italian and they got along famously.

The prosecuting attorney's name was Mark. He was a young man in his mid to late twenties. He was of medium height and build. He didn't appear arrogant or hateful. He had brown hair, and brown eyes. Mark looked like an ordinary guy doing an ordinary job.

3

The courtroom had no audience. The room had wood walls, chairs, desks, and floors. A warm yet very cold atmosphere filled the room.

My attorney gave me a little background of Judge Ray who would be presiding. He was appointed to the bench in the early eighties. He was a fair judge, not hard or soft. He was a Captain in the Navy in his early years. Judge Ray entered the room.

"All stand," the Bailiff said.

Judge Ray was of medium height. His black robe covered his build. He was older, with whiter than white hair. We all were seated.

Judge Ray explained the reason for this first appearance to the court. U.S. Coast Guard Boatswain, Huey would take the stand first.

Huey took the stand, under oath. Huey was in his early twenties. He looked as if he lifted weights at some time in his life. He was a stocky guy, with blond hair, and brown eyes. His declaration went like this:

I, Huey, hereby declare and state:

I'm a member of the United States Coast Guard Pacific Area Tactical Team (PACAREA TACLET), and am presently assigned as a Boarding Officer. The facts set forth herein are personally known by me to be true and correct, and, if called as a witness, I could competently testify thereto.

On March 23, 1992, the PACAREA TACLET was on patrol aboard the USS Vincennes off the coast of Mexico. We had previously been advised that an electronic tracking device had been installed on a United States registered sailing vessel. The vessel, which the Federal Bureau of Investigation believed was being used to transport narcotics from Mexico to Southern California.´ We were further advised that the vessel contained hidden compartments, including one in its aft area.

At approximately 1:00 a.m., we determined the general vicinity of the vessel with the aid of the tracking device. Our support helicopter searched the area and located several vessels. One recreational vessel was heading north across the mouth of a bay. Given the time of day, we considered this course highly suspicious. Based on this suspicious course, and the fact that the vessel was in international waters, we decided to board the vessel.

Prior to boarding the vessel, the officer in charge of our unit, Lieutenant Gay, announced our intention to board, and asked the Master of the vessel a series of routine preboarding questions, including the names and dates of birth of all parties on board. The Master later identified as Paul, provided his name and birthdate, as well as the name and birthdate of the sole passenger AKA DOCTOR.

The boarding team consisted of Boatswain Dewey, Boatswain Louie, and me Boatswain Huey. As we approached the vessel, I noticed that the back of the vessel appeared to be riding low in the water. Immediately upon boarding the vessel, the boarding team conducted and initial safety inspection (ISI). After completing the ISI, I began the standard document and safety inspection of the vessel with Paul, using the Coast Guard 4100 form.

Part of the safety inspection involves my inspecting all bilge spaces and trace out engine compartments to determine whether there is an accumulation of water or fuel. During this inspection, I discovered an area of unaccounted space under a row of bench seats on the deck of the vessel. There appeared to be an area of fiberglass material, which did not match the fiberglass in the other portions of the vessel, which I had inspected. At approximately the same time, Dewey noticed what appeared to be new wooden trim work in the cabin of the vessel. This trim work appeared less worn than the other woodwork on the vessel. Moreover, the screws holding the trim in place were shiny and clean. The other screws and woodwork in the area were worn and dirty. It appeared to both Dewey and me that work had recently been done to that area of the vessel. I asked both Paul and the Doctor whether any work had been done on the vessel. Both men said no work had been done.

During the inspection, Dewey told me that he believed Paul acted nervously when we inspected the area around the trim work. At approximately the same time I received word from Lieutenant Gay that an EPIC check based on the personal information provided by Paul prior to boarding revealed a prior narcotics smuggling conviction, and that the passengers on board the vessel were to be considered armed and dangerous.

Based upon all these factors, I decided to remove the wooden trim to determine whether it concealed any hidden compartment. I asked Paul if he would provide us with a screwdriver to remove the trim. Paul provided a screwdriver, which Dewey used to remove the trim. When he removed the trim, a fiberglass panel behind the trim fell away. Behind the panel was another fiberglass panel surrounded by duct tape. Dewey removed the second panel, revealing a large hidden compartment containing approximately 30 bundles of marijuana. We later removed other panels in the area, ultimately finding six other hidden compartments and 73 additional bundles of marijuana.

Huey stepped from the witness stand. He looked over at me and grinned. I smiled back knowing this was just the start of this chess game. The prosecutor, Mark, stated the following legality of the use of a tracking device.

I'm the Assistant United States Attorney assigned the prosecution of this case.

On September 18, 1991, the Honorable Judge Judy, signed an order authorizing the installation and use of a tracking device on the sailing vessel Driven, to aid physical

6

surveillance operations of the vessel. Judge Judy ordered that the application, affidavit and order authorizing the use of the tracking device be sealed until further order of the court. True and correct copies of the application, affidavit, order and order for sealing are attached hereto as Exhibit 1.

On February 13, 1992, the government sought a further order authorizing the continued use of the tracking device previously installed in the vessel. Judge Judy signed another order authorizing the government to continue to operate the tracking device for an additional ninety days, or until the conclusion of the investigation. True and correct copies of the supplemental application, affidavit, and order are attached hereto as Exhibit 2.

On July 30, 1992, I spoke by telephone with Lieutenant Gay. I reviewed with him in detail the attached declaration of Lieutenant Gay, which I had previously sent to him via telecopier. Lieutenant Gay indicated that the declaration was accurate in all respects, and expressed his intention to sign the declaration prior to the time for hearing on this matter.

We all stood when the judge finally left the courtroom. Paul and I were immediately handcuffed and escorted by the Marshal's to our holding cell in the lower level.

Before we left the courtroom, our attorney's said they would be in contact with us.

While waiting to be taken back to MDC, Paul and I tried to figure out what the hell a tracking device was doing on board Driven? There must have been an informant? We had no idea. The entire operation was only four people. Paul and I were two of them. We were never asked for any kind of information, nor did we offer any. Our minds raced as we were driven back to MDC.

METROPOLITAN DETENTION CENTER

We were settling in at our new home on the ninth floor. MDC was ten stories tall. On different floors throughout the building housed over one thousand inmates. There was a segregation area, female prisoner area, foodservice, and counseling, visiting area. Each unit held one hundred thirty inmates. Our unit had two floors, with two man cells. Each cell had iron pan beds, with two-inch plastic mattresses, and a plastic pillow. The four inch wide, four-foot tall thick window provided us a view of Union Station and Alameda Street.

I could tell a million stories of the people we met inside that unit. The common area had a Universal weight-training machine in the outside area. This outside area was covered with iron bars above, and cement walls on the side. Smokers could smoke out there, and there was a basketball hoop.

The inside common area had stainless steel tables with benches to seat us all. Games of cards, chess, and the slapping of dominoes on the stainless tables could be heard for miles. A guard's desk sat next to the exit door. Every guard on duty never got in the way of any activity. They were there to call for help if any violence broke out. Violence did break out weekly.

At ten o'clock each night we were locked inside our cells. At six o'clock every morning our doors were unlocked for daily activity. If you had a court appearance, you get up at four in the morning to make it to your appointment. Appointments started at nine in the morning, and ended at five in the afternoon. You still get up at four in the morning.

Our families and friends knew of our problem. My parents understood from past experience. Paul's family found it hard to deal with. My girlfriend Meg knew from experience that this was part of the game. You learn to play this game with no rules.

Day's later Paul's family put up the two hundred and fifty thousand dollar bail for him. We shook hands as he left the unit. The steel door slammed behind him. I was not alone. My cribbage partner Charlie, was waiting for me at the stainless table. Fifteen two, fifteen four, and there ain't no more.

Paul had been gone for two weeks when I got a visit from my attorney. I was escorted down to the visiting room. We had a private attorney client room. Reed told me the prosecutor had made him an offer for Paul and me. Plead Guilty and get five years each. This was a great deal for me being a second time offender. I was looking at ten years easily. Paul was looking at what he would be getting anyway. I asked him why the deal? He said the FBI didn't want to expose the informant, because the informant was working on another case, and didn't want me or us to know who it was.

"Informant?" I asked sternly.

"There is an informant in your case. He was being paid by the FBI," Reed said. "If you take the deal, you will have to figure out who it is on your own. Regardless, whoever it is will be long gone by the time you get out after eighty five percent of five years," Reed explained.

"I'll take it," I said.

"Now, we will find out if Paul will take it. I will let you know," Reed said as he left.

My mind raced as I was escorted back to my unit. I couldn't believe it. Eduardo was in Mexico, he couldn't be. John had family and friends all over Minneapolis. He couldn't be. I thought to myself.

Two days later I called Paul on the phone, and he finally answered.

9

"No, I'm not taking the deal, Doctor. My attorney says we are going to beat this thing. He is good, Doctor," Paul said.

"Paul, there is an informant. You go to trial, and he testifies, and the jury believes him, you still do five," I said.

"We can beat this Doctor. I like being free out here. I have a girlfriend now," he said.

"You have only been out for a couple weeks. Now you have a girlfriend? Geez, man, start thinking with your big head," I said.

Well, Paul was convinced that we would beat this thing. I had to go along, because it was a joint deal. Both of us sign, or no deal. My signature was now void.

Reed told me we were going to set a trial date. I was going to trial separately from Paul. Reed said he would contact me when he had more discovery in the case. He would bring me the name of the informant soon. The informant would have to testify now. I was going to get ten years mandatory minimum if I plead guilty now, or went to trial. Mandatory/Minimum sentencing held all the cards.

A week later Reed came to see me. I was escorted down to the visiting room. Reed had his brief case open setting on the wooden table.

"Do you know a guy named Ben Crump--r?" he asked saying the last name.

"I was in prison with him back in nineteen eighty-three," I said.

"He is the paid informant. He has been informing for years now. He even put his brother and son in jail on drug charges," Reed said.

"I don't understand?" I said.

"Ben says you called him and offered him a deal. He says you told him you would contact him after you finished this deal you were working on. He told the FBI that you were planning a smuggle, and they started paying him. He was the reason for the tracking device on board. He says he knew where the hidden compartments were," Reed said.

"He never stepped foot on the boat," I exclaimed. "I told him no to his deal that he offered me. I did say I had a prior engagement, and that I would get back to him when I got back," I explained.

"That is all it took," he said.

"So, what's next?" I asked.

"Paul is going to plead guilty to the five years he has coming anyway. You go to jury trial, and we try to beat this rat informant into the ground," Reed said. "You get ten years, if you plead, or go to trial. Let's go to trial," he said smiling.

"I'm in," I said.

I was escorted back to my unit. We would get a trial date, and start by picking a jury. I couldn't wait to call Paul.

"I'm sorry, Doctor, I'm sorry. Man, I didn't know," Paul, said almost crying.

"I didn't know either you jerk," I said.

Paul and I hung up from the conversation on a good note. I played the game; I have to deal with it. Paul's new girlfriend had already left him for some cocaine dealer in Long Beach.

THE TRIAL

The courtroom was filled with soon to be jurors. Black, White, Spanish. People of all ages looked around the room, and at me. Reed started the interviews, the prosecutor followed. I was asked to stand, and turn around for the jurors to view me. I wore dark blue khaki pants, with a flowered print shirt. No suit and tie for me today.

After a couple hours Reed, the prosecutor, and myself were pleased with the selection. Five white guys between the ages of forty and sixty. Two black ladies between the ages of twenty and thirty. Two elderly white ladies. There were three Hispanic men ranging in age between forty and fifty. The alternate juror was a white male, my age wearing a black leather coat. I truly believed I had a chance.

"What now?" I asked Reed.

"The trial starts at one thirty today," he answered.

I was escorted back to the holding cell. The jurors were taken away for instructions.

Soon it would be showtime. I ate an apple for lunch, and tried to relax. I had the holding cell to myself. I wanted to sleep, go to a movie, and sleep with Meg, anything but this. I was able to rest until the Marshal's came for me.

I was escorted back to the courtroom. I passed a small room that Ben was sitting in. He looked away quickly. Inside the courtroom had the Customs agents, FBI agents, Coast Guard people, and assorted others waiting. They all cleared out when I came in. They would now go wait outside the door until they were called to testify.

LOS ANGELES, CALIFORNIA; TUESDAY, NOVEMBER 10, 1992; 1:30 PM.

The Court: At this time ladies and gentlemen, the clerk is going to hand each of you a notebook and a pencil. You are not required to take notes, but sometimes it is helpful to refresh your memory later during deliberations.

Prosecutor Mark. You may call your first witness.

Mark: Your honor, the government calls Benjamin Crump--r.

The Clerk: Will you raise your right hand. 'He is sworn in, and seated.

Mark: Ben, do you know the defendant, the Doctor.

Ben: Yes I do.

Mark: Could you point at him and tell us what he is wearing.

Ben: He is wearing a flowered shirt sitting at that table.

Mark: Your honor the record should reflect that the witness has pointed to the defendant.

The Court: So shall it be recorded.

Mark: When did you first meet the defendant?

Ben: 1984.

Mark: Did you speak with him during late 1990?

Ben: Yes I did.

Mark: Did you phone him?

Ben: No, he phoned me.

Mark: Where were you when he called?

Ben: At my mother's home. I live with my mother in Fort Worth, Texas.

Mark: Do you know where he was calling from?

Reed: Objection. Calls for a conclusion. No foundation.

The Court: Well, I think you are one question ahead of it. The answer to this is yes or no. Does he know? So you may answer. The objection to this question is overruled, but the answer should be yes or no.

Ben: Yes.

Mark: Did he tell you were he was calling from?

Reed: Objection. Calls for hearsay, your honor. Also no foundation.

The Court: Well, foundation is correct. Sustained on that. There is no foundation set for this.

Mark: Did he tell you why he was calling you?

Ben: He said he wanted to—

The Court: No, No. Yes or no.

Ben: Yes.

Mark: What did he say?

Ben: That he would like to come and see me.

Mark: Did he tell you why he wanted to come and see you?

Ben: No.

Mark: Did you agree to meet with him?

Ben: Yes.

Mark: Did you meet him shortly after the conversation?

Ben: Yes.

Mark: Where?

Ben: Fort Worth, Texas at a hotel.

Mark: What did you discuss at this meeting?

Ben: We discussed the Doctor's ability to smuggle marijuana.

Mark: Did he discuss any plans with you?

Reed: Objection. Leading the witness.

The Court: Sustained.

Mark: What do you mean when you say you discussed his ability?

Ben: The Doctor informed me that he had been working with other groups, he had been selling marijuana and would like to get, would like to make another trip of marijuana or drugs to sell.

Mark: Did you agree to smuggle drugs with him at that meeting?

Ben: No.

Mark: Had you been involved in drug smuggling before the Doctor called you?

Ben: Yes.

Mark: When?

Ben: From a period of 1974 until 1984.

Mark: Were you ever convicted of any drug related crime?

Ben: Yes, I was.

Mark: When.

Ben: In 1985 or 1986, and again in 1987.

Mark: Were you sentenced to prison?

Ben: Yes.

Mark: Did you serve time in prison?

Ben: Yes, I did.

Mark: When were you released from prison?

Ben: 1990

Mark: How soon before that call that you've referred to in late 1990 were you released from prison?

Ben: I would have just been released. I was still in a halfway house, Federal halfway house.

Mark: At that time, were you interested in engaging in further drug smuggling activity?

Ben: No.

Mark: Did you tell the defendant that you were not interested in smuggling drugs?

Reed: Objection. Relevancy.

The Court: Sustained.

Mark: Did you meet with the defendant again after your initial meeting in Fort Worth?

Ben: Yes.

Mark: How many times?

Ben: I can't recall, but it was several times.

Mark: More than five times?

Ben: A total of five times.

Mark: During what time period?

Ben: From late 1990 until August of September 1991.

Mark: During that time period, did you receive calls from anyone other than the defendant about engaging in drug smuggling?

Reed: Objection. Relevancy. Also calls for hearsay.

The Court: Sustained.

Mark: What did you do in response to the inquiries from the defendant regarding drug smuggling?

Ben: I informed the defendant that I would check into it to see if I could help him in any way.

Mark: Did you do anything else?

Ben: I eventually called the FBI.

Mark: When did you call the FBI?

Ben: I don't recall if it was April or May of 1991.

Mark: What did you tell the FBI agents?

Ben: I told them that I had been contacted by two different organizations that were interested in smuggling drugs, that I had no intention of doing it, and I didn't know what to do, and what should I do at this point.

Mark: Did the agents show an interest in having you cooperate with them?

Ben: Yes.

Mark: Did you begin working with them?

Ben: Yes.

Mark: When?

Ben: August of 1991.

Mark: Did you have any sort of financial arrangement with the FBI?

Ben: Yes.

Mark: What was the arrangement?

Ben: That they would pay me $5,000.00 per month, plus expenses.

Mark: What were you to do in exchange for the money?

Ben: I was to travel extensively for them, give them intelligence information regarding several organizations and cooperate fully in any investigation, as well as testify in any court proceedings.

Mark: Were you instructed to work with any particular agent?

Ben: Yes.

Mark: In what part of the country?

Ben: Los Angeles, California.

Mark: Are you still working with the FBI?

Ben: No.

Mark: When did you stop working for them?

Ben: July 1992.

Mark: Did the FBI pay you the $5,000.00 per month?

Ben: Yes.

Mark: Between August of 1991 and July of 1992, approximately how much did the FBI pay you?

Ben: Approximately 40 to $45,000.00 dollars.

Mark: Did they reimburse expenses?

Ben: Yes.

Mark: What were the nature if those expenses?

Ben: Flights to and from South America, hotels, telephone calls, etc.

Mark: How much did they reimburse you?

Ben: About $40,000.00 dollars.

Mark: When you began working with the FBI in August of 1991, did the FBI agents instruct you to keep in contact with the defendant?

Ben: Yes.

Mark: Did you.

Ben: Yes.

Mark: Did you meet with the defendant after you began working with the FBI?

Ben: Yes.

Mark: Where?

Ben: Long Beach, California.

Mark: How many meetings did you have with the defendant in Long Beach, after you began working with the FBI?

Ben: Two, possibly three. I don't recall.

Mark: During those meetings, did you have any further discussions with the defendant about drug smuggling?

Ben: Yes.

Mark: What was the general nature of those discussions?

Reed: Objection. Calls for a narrative.

The Court: Sustained.

Mark: Were the discussions that you had with the defendant similar to the discussions you had with him previously in Texas?

Reed: Objection. Calls for a conclusion.

The Court: Overruled.

Ben: Yes.

Mark: Did the defendant describe any specific plans that he had for drug smuggling?

Ben: Yes.

Mark: What were those plans?

Ben: He informed that he was willing to go anywhere to bring back a load of drugs. He first had to finish the obligation he had, and after that he would be willing to work with me.

Mark: Did he describe that obligation to you?

Ben: Yes.

Mark: What was that obligation?

Ben: He informed that he was to bring back a load of marijuana within a sailboat, and that he was going to conceal the marijuana within the sailboat.

Mark: Did he tell you where the marijuana was ultimately going to be delivered?

Ben: Yes. To the Long Beach area.

Mark: Did the defendant show you the boat?

Ben: Yes.

Mark: Your honor, at this time I request permission to place Exhibit 1 before the witness.

The Court: Yes. Don't publish it before the jury, before it's received into evidence. Turn the backside so the jury isn't looking at it.

Mark: Do you recognize Exhibit 1?

Ben: Yes.

Mark: What is it?

Ben: A 35 or 36-foot sailboat.

Mark: Is that the sailboat the defendant showed you?

Ben: Yes.

Mark: I move government's Exhibit 1 into evidence.

The Court: It will be received.

Mark: Did the defendant show you where on the boat he was planning to store drugs?

Ben: Yes.

Mark: Had hidden compartments been installed?

Reed: Objection. Calls for a conclusion.

The Court: Sustained.

Reed: No foundation.

The Court: In that form.

Mark: When was the last time you met the defendant?

Ben: Late September 1991.

Mark: Where?

Ben: At a bar in Long Beach.

Mark: What did you and the defendant discuss at that meeting?

Ben: The defendant informed me that he had a lot of police surveillance on him, and that he was possibly going to move the boat, and that he couldn't work with me. He said when he got done with this obligation he would contact me.

Mark: Did you have any part in setting up the obligation you refer to?

Reed: Objection. Calls for a conclusion, also relevancy.

The Court: Read the question back.

The Court: Overruled. You may answer.

Ben: No.

Mark: Do you know who the sellers of the drugs were?

Ben: No.

Reed: Objection. No foundation.

The Court: He is asking if he knows. Overruled.

Mark: Did you have any contact with either the buyer or the seller of the marijuana?

Ben: No.

Mark: Between late September 1991 and July of 1992, did any of your work with the FBI relate to the investigation of the defendant?

Ben: No.

Mark: No further questions.

The Court: All right. Reed you may examine.

CROSS-EXAMINATION

Reed: Before coming into court today, did you have a chance to review any kind of notes?

Ben: No.

Reed: Did you review any kind of Police Reports?

Ben: No.

Reed: Did you review any kind of documents?

Ben: Uh, yes.

Reed: Were the documents in the nature of the investigation reports?

Ben: Uh, yes.

Reed: And this incident, you're interacting with the Doctor, occurred back in 1990 or 1991?

Ben: Yes.

Reed: And before coming into court to testify, were these notes you reviewed given to you by anybody?

Ben: Yes.

Reed: Is that person present in court today?

Ben: Yes.

Reed: Was he the Assistant United States Attorney on the case?

Ben: Yes.

Reed: Mark, correct?

Ben: Yes.

Reed: And he was meeting with you to prepare you for trial, to testify?

Ben: Yes.

Reed: In the course of that meeting to prepare you for the testimony, he handed you some documents?

Ben: A single document.

Reed: Pardon?

Ben: A single document.

Reed: How many times have you met with Mark to prepare your testimony?

Ben: One time.

Reed: When was that?

Ben: Yesterday.

Reed: Were you in the presence of an FBI agent at that time?

Ben: Yes.

Reed: What was the name of the agent?

Ben: Tim.

Reed: Did Tim supervise your work?

Ben: Yes.

Reed: He was known as your supervising agent?

Ben: I don't know the name. Uh, yes I would assume so.

Reed: You were released from prison, when?

Ben: 1990

Reed: After serving your full term?

Ben: Yes.

Reed: When you were released from prison in 1990, had you been giving any information at all before that date to any kind of law enforcement agents?

Ben: No.

Reed: In 1990 you were placed in a halfway house; is that correct?

Ben: Yes.

Reed: The halfway was in the Texas area?

Ben: Yes.

Reed: You had been up to this point of 1990 convicted of what offenses?

Ben: Of marijuana smuggling and possession of marijuana.

Reed: Two separate convictions?

Ben: I believe so, yes.

Reed: One conviction was in 1985, correct?

Ben: I don't recall.

Reed: On that particular prosecution, was there—had you skipped on your bail?

Ben: Yes.

Reed: And you were arrested on that case in which you were convicted in what year?

Ben: 1984—Originally arrested in 1974.

Reed: And you were brought to court on that arrest; right?

Ben: Yes.

Reed: Which state were you arrested.

Ben: Indiana.

Reed: When you were brought into court, you received a bail in that case; correct?

Ben: Yes.

Reed: And the nature of that prosecution was marijuana; correct?

Ben: Yes.

Reed: It was a distribution of marijuana case?

Ben: Yes.

Reed: It was a felony offense?

Ben: Yes.

Reed: How much was the bail?

Ben: I do not recall.

Reed: After you were brought into court that very first time, a bail was arranged in your case; correct?

Ben: Yes.

Reed: And when was it that you left the jurisdiction, or I should say when was it that you skipped out on your bail in that particular prosecution?

Ben: 1975.

Reed: So had you been making your court appearances for approximately six months to a year before you skipped out on your bail?

Ben: Approximately three months.

Reed: Who posted your bail?

Ben: My wife.

Reed: And what was the bail in your matter?

Ben: I don't recall, I believe it was $50,000, but, uh, it was a long time ago.

Reed: And how long were you a fugitive until you were arrested?

Ben: In excess of ten years.

Reed: Now, you knew when you skipped out on bail, the person who had raised the bail was going to lose the money; correct?

Ben: That's correct.

Reed: That's what bail is all about; correct?

Ben: Yes.

Now, when you were arrested after remaining at large for a good period of time, were you arrested on some new type of charge?

Ben: Yes.

Reed: And what was the nature of that offense?

Ben: It was a conspiracy to import and distribute cocaine.

Reed: And when you were arrested on that, the police department ran a warrant check on you and they determined that you were also a fugitive on this other marijuana offense; correct?

Mark: Objection. Call for speculation.

The Court: Sustained.

Reed: When you taken into custody on this new case, the police indicated to you that they knew that you had been a fugitive?

Ben: Yes.

Reed: In what state where you taken into custody on the new case?

Ben: I was arrested in Georgia, but I was extradited to Florida, the Federal Middle District.

Reed: On the new case?

Ben: Yes.

Reed: Now, on that other case that you were arrested on, the newer one, were you eventually returned to the jurisdiction in which you fled?

Ben: Yes.

Reed: And in that particular case, you eventually entered a plea of guilty in that particular prosecution; true.

Ben: Yes.

Reed: And that was the marijuana case; right?

Ben: Yes.

Reed: In 1987, you were eventually convicted on the new case that you had picked up, which was a cocaine case; correct?

Ben: No.

Reed: You were eventually convicted on this case in which you were arrested on as a fugitive; true?

Ben: Yes.

Reed: What year did you enter a plea in that case?

Ben: 1986.

Reed: And that was a cocaine case; right?

Ben: No.

Reed: What type of case was that?

Ben: That was a marijuana case.

Reed: Was that down in Florida?

Ben: No.

Reed: Where was that case?

Ben: Indiana.

Reed: You were eventually arrested on another case involving cocaine; is that true?

Ben: I was arrested at that time—I was picked up on the fugitive warrant for the cocaine case, yes.

Reed: okay. Now, after being released into a halfway house, there came a point in time when the Doctor telephoned you; right.

Ben: Yes.

Reed: And he reached you at your mother's house in Texas?

Ben: Yes.

Reed: And when you met with the Doctor, you would meet him dressed in street clothes; true?

Ben: Yes.

Reed: When you were working with the FBI in an undercover capacity, you would generally wear street clothes; correct?

Ben: Yes.

Reed: Today, I notice you are wearing a suit to testify on court; correct?

Ben: Yes.

Reed: Now, did agent Tim suggest to you that when you came to testify before the jury in our case, that you dress up in a suit?

Ben: I volunteered that.

Reed: That was your idea?

Ben: It was my idea.

Reed: Did you think that you would have perhaps a more sincere demeanor before the jury by wearing a suit?

Ben: Yes.

Reed: When you received the phone call from the Doctor, you traveled to Fort Worth, Texas; correct?

Ben: I was living with my mother in Fort Worth.

Reed: Did you meet the Doctor in Fort Worth?

Ben: Yes.

Reed: And the first time you met the Doctor in Fort Worth, had you become involved with the FBI?

Ben: No.

Reed: Had you become involved with any kind of police agency whatsoever up to that point in time?

Ben: No.

Reed: You did provide any information as what's known as an informant up until that first point in time that you met with the Doctor?

Ben: No.

Reed: After meeting with the Doctor, you decided that you would go to the FBI; correct?

Ben: After several meetings, yes.

Reed: And did you feel a sense of community conscience that led you to go to the FBI?

Ben: No.

Reed: Where were you working at that time?

Ben: With a construction company.

Reed: And you were making how much per month?

Ben: approximately $1,500 per month.

Reed: You went to the FBI at that point in time because you felt that you could make more money as an informant; correct?

Ben: No.

Reed: When you went to the FBI, whom did you meet with that very first time?

Mark: Objection, irrelevant.

The Court: I can't tell. Is this going to be tied up in some way?

Reed: Your Honor, I can withdraw the question.

The Court: All right.

Reed: Did you decide which police agency you wanted to work with after meeting with the Doctor?

Ben: I decided which agency I would call. I did not know whether I would work with them or what I would do, but I felt more comfortable calling the people I called.

Reed: When you came into contact with the FBI you gave them some information; correct?

Ben: Yes.

Reed: And you didn't do it because you were interested in getting the money; right?

Ben: No.

Reed: And you didn't do it out of a sense of community concern; correct?

Ben: No.

Reed: Then after giving information at that point in time to the FBI, did the FBI indicate to you that they wanted to put you on a payroll of some type?

Ben: Eventually, yes.

Reed: And from the point in time that you first came to the FBI until the point in time, which you in your mind thought you were going to be paid for information, how much time went by?

Ben: Four or five months.

Reed: And how much did the FBI say that they were going to pay you?

Ben: An agreement was eventually reached, at $5,000.00 per month.

Reed: Was there any discussion with the FBI to the effect that the more information you gave to them, the more they would pay you?

Ben: No.

Reed: You in your mind thought you were going to be getting $5,000.00 per month regardless of the amount of information that you gave to the FBI; is that right?

Ben: I can only assume that evaluated the information I was giving them, and they felt it was worth that. It was not negotiated; it was a figure they gave me.

Reed: When was the very first month you went to work for the FBI in which you were paid?

Ben: September or October.

Reed: Of which year.

Ben: 1991.

Reed: And you had been interacting with the FBI for several months before that particular month; correct.

Ben: Yes.

Reed: They weren't paying you during those months; correct?

Ben: No. They had paid me expense money to travel and talk to them.

Reed: Did you feel in your mind that the more information you provided the larger amount of money per month would be provided?

Ben: No.

Reed: Did there come a point in time during your interaction with the FBI where you in your mind thought that it was about time the FBI made a decision to pay you?

Ben: That was voluntary on the FBI. I did not bring it up.

Reed: So it is fair to say that you had been working with the FBI for months, and you weren't even concerned about being paid?

Ben: The only time I felt concerned was when it became impossible to continue with my job; I couldn't because of the traveling. At that point, I told them that I either had to quit or something had to be done, that I could not continue taking off work in doing this. And that was when they told me they would, uh, they came up with this figure for me.

Reed: And that would have been in September or October 1991; correct?

Ben: To the best of my recollection.

Reed: And which agent did you interact with at that time? Agent Tim?

Ben: No.

Mark: Objection. Irrelevant. And move to strike the witness's answer.

The Court: Overruled. The answer will stand.

Reed: Now, in September 1991, after working with the FBI for a few months, there came a point in time when you came to California and met with the Doctor; is that right?

Ben: Yes.

Reed: And approximately how many times had you come into contact with FBI agents before September of 1991?

Ben: A dozen.

Reed: And in terms of the nature of the relationship you told the FBI that you had with the Doctor, it was one wherein you two were friends; correct?

Ben: Yes.

Reed: In other words, you told the FBI that the Doctor is a friend of mine, and he knows who I'am; right?

Ben: Yes.

Reed: You told the FBI that "I have spoken to the Doctor on several occasions; correct?

Ben: Yes.

Reed: Now, you knew that the FBI had available to it various tools that they use in the investigation of cases; true?

Ben: I don't understand, I don't understand?

Reed: You had been involved in the narcotic trade for some time before 1991; correct?

Ben: Yes.

Reed: You had a couple of convictions, and had gone to prison; true?

Ben: Yes.

Reed: You interacted with other prison inmates while you were serving your sentence; correct?

Ben: Yes.

Reed: And you knew for example, that the FBI had available to it tape recorders that they could use?

Ben: Yes.

Reed: And you knew that the FBI had available to it what are known as transmitting devices; correct?

Ben: Yes.

Reed: And you knew that the FBI had available to them what are known as wire transmitters; right?

Ben: Yes.

Reed: Where you wear a wire; correct?

Ben: I had heard of that.

Reed: And you had known that before September 1991; right?

Ben: Yes.

Reed: Could you explain to the jury what it means to wear a wire transmitter on your person in a hidden location so that they can understand what a wire transmitter is?

Ben: Well, I'm certainly no expert. I have never done it. I can only tell you what I have seen in the movies.

Reed: Now, could you tell us what a wire transmitter is?

Ben: I can only assume it is a tape recorder that is put on your body with a microphone that would receive any conversation or sounds and it could be recorded.

Reed: And you know the FBI also has available to it the ability to tape record telephone conversations as well; right?

Ben: Yes.

Reed: In other words, a person could call an informant who may happen to be by a telephone, and the informant could use a tape recorder in which to tape record that conversation; right?

Ben: Yes.

Reed: Right?

Ben: Yes, that's correct.

Reed: Now, over the course of several months before September of 1991, you say that you had interacted with the Doctor on several occasions; correct?

Ben: Yes.

Reed: And you had already been working with the FBI for several months before September of 1991; correct?

Ben: Yes.

Reed: You had had up to September 1991 various telephone conversations with the Doctor; correct?

Ben: Yes.

Reed: And then in September of 1991, the FBI knew that you were going to be meeting with the Doctor at a location where this boat was located; right?

Mark: Objection. Calls for speculation.

The Court: Sustained.

Reed: Did you tell the agents that you were going to be meeting him at the area where his boat was located?

Ben: Yes.

Reed: Now, this boat was not owned by the Doctor; isn't that true?

Ben: I don't know.

Reed: Now when you talked with the Doctor over the telephone during the totality of the period of time in which you had conversations with him, did you ever tape record one conversation?

Ben: Yes.

Reed: With the Doctor?

Ben: Yes.

Reed: And there was a tape-recorded conversation with the Doctor that the FBI has?

Ben: Yes, I believe so.

Reed: And during the entire period of time that you interacted with the Doctor, you had met with him on several occasions; correct?

Ben: Yes.

Reed: And when you met with the Doctor on these occasions, you would come into personal contact with him; right?

Ben: Yes.

Reed: And he would not be very far away from you while you talked to him during these occasions; right?

Ben: No.

Reed: Within arm's length of each other you would talk to him; right?

Ben: Yes.

Reed: And would it be fair to say that you would spend a certain amount of time with him during these occasions?

Ben: Usually a half hour to an hour.

Reed: During any of these periods of time in which you were in the Doctors immediate presence, did you ever wear a wire on your person?

Ben: No.

Reed: Were you in the presence of an undercover FBI agent at any time when you interacted with the Doctor?

Ben: No.

Reed: During the entire time that you interacted with the Doctor in Long Beach in September 1991, was it just you interacting with him?

Ben: There were other people present.

Reed: The other person that was present was Paul?

Ben: Yes.

Mark: Objection. Vague as to time or place of meeting. Which meeting.

The Court: Sustained.

Reed: In September of 1991, is it fair to say that you met with the Doctor three or four times?

Ben: I don't know the exact number, no. At least two times.

Reed: And during this period of time, there was another individual on any of these three occasions, two or three occasions, another individual who was in the immediate presence of the Doctor; right?

Ben: Yes.

Reed: And this person was Paul?

Ben: Yes.

Reed: Did you speak with Paul during these meetings?

Ben: Yes.

Reed: Now, were you with anybody during the course of these two or three meetings?

Ben: No.

Reed: Were you driven to these meetings by an FBI agent, let off a block away, would you walk to these meetings and then report back to the agent?

Ben: No.

Reed: When you went to these meetings during September of 1991, did you tell the agents that you were going to the meetings?

Ben: Yes.

Reed: And after the meetings were over, you would come back to—you would report back to the FBI concerning what the nature of the interaction was; right?

Ben: Yes.

Reed: Did they tape record any of those meetings between yourself and the FBI?

Ben: No.

Reed: Is it fair to say that the information that the FBI had concerning the Doctor was based solely on what you had told them?

Mark: Objection. Calls for speculation.

The Court: Sustained.

Reed: Now, you know that the FBI has available to it cameras; right?

Ben: Yes.

Reed: Cameras that they can use in an undercover capacity and take photographs of things; right?

Ben: Yes.

Reed: Were you provided with any kind of camera by the FBI?

Ben: No.

Reed: After September of 1991, did you ever meet with the Doctor again?

Ben: No.

Reed: It is fair to say then that the meetings that did take place between you and him in the Long Beach area all occurred during the month of September 1991; right?

Ben: I don't know exactly.

Reed: Now, during the course of some of these meetings, they occurred in an area where a sailboat was located; right?

Ben: Yes.

Reed: And did you, after the meetings were over, ever go back with the FBI, for example, at night, and go on board this sailboat with the FBI at any time?

Ben: No.

Reed: When you saw this sailboat which is depicted in Exhibit 1 for the first time, do you recall whether or not the sailboat, if you know or not, was made out of fiberglass, wood, metal, what the nature of the material was that the boat was made out of?

Ben: Fiberglass.

Reed: Now, this other person, Paul, was present during some of these meetings that you had in September of 1991?

Ben: Yes.

Reed: Was he present do you recall during the first meeting?

Ben: I believe so.

Reed: Was that the first time you ever saw Paul?

Ben: Yes.

Reed: The Doctor introduced you to Paul at that meeting?

Ben: Yes.

Reed: Did Paul ever give you information to the effect that the sailboat was his, that he was the owner in the sailboat?

Ben: Yes.

Reed: And during the second meeting that you had, do you know if Paul was present?

Ben: I had a meeting in which the Doctor was not present and Paul was.

Reed: And during the course of that meeting Paul discussed with you the fact that he was going to be importing marijuana; correct?

Ben: He informed me, I think, that he was going to be one of two or three people, yes.

Reed: Now, was the first meeting that occurred when you were introduced to Paul at the sailboat?

Ben: Yes.

Reed: And where was the sailboat located at that time?

Ben: Long Beach, California.

Reed: And the second meeting was at the same location?

Ben: I believe it was at an apartment in Long Beach.

Reed: And the third meeting?

Ben: Also in an apartment.

Reed: The fourth meeting?

Ben: I don't know that there was a fourth meeting. The fourth meeting I believe was at a bar in Long Beach.

Reed: Where did you meet Paul by himself?

Ben: I didn't meet with him by myself.

Reed: Where was this meeting when you were interacting with just Paul?

Ben: In an apartment.

Reed: In the city of Long Beach.

Ben: Yes.

Reed: Again no wire was worn by you?

Ben: No.

Reed: You know what I mean when I say wire?

Ben: Yes.

Reed: A transmitting device that is hidden on your person so that other people can hear what you are saying; right?

Ben: Yes.

Reed: In September you were making this $5,000.00 per month; correct?

Ben: I think it started in October. I think I was paid retroactively.

Reed: And after September of 1991, September or October, you say you were paid in terms of total amount of benefits, or total amount of money by the FBI, a sum approximately $90,000?

Ben: I was paid $45,000.

Reed: Cash?

Ben: For myself. Yes. And the rest of it was for expenses.

Reed: And the money the FBI paid you was claimed on your income taxes?

Ben: Yes.

Reed: The FBI told you that it was income and that you would have to report that money; correct?

Ben: Yes.

Reed: Now, after September of 1991, you started to receive your $5,000 on a monthly basis; correct?

Ben: Yes.

Reed: And how many months did you continue to work for the FBI until you stopped working for them?

Ben: I stopped working in July of 1992.

Reed: Now, you were subpoenaed to come to the court today to testify; correct?

Ben: Yes.

Reed: Did FBI agent Tim subpoena you?

Ben: I believe the United States Government subpoenaed me. I don't know.

Reed: Who gave you the subpoena?

Ben: The Assistant U.S. Attorney.

Reed: Who called you to come down to the Assistant United States Attorney's Office?

Ben: Agent Tim.

Reed: I take it agent Tim has been keeping in touch with you over the last four months?

Ben: Yes.

Reed: Did agent Tim indicate to you, words to the effect that part of your obligation is to come and testify in the Federal Court?

Ben: Yes.

Reed: Are you currently employed?

Ben: No.

Reed: And you are not being paid by the FBI at the present time; correct?

Ben: That's correct.

Reed: Are you being paid by any other police agencies at this time?

Ben: No.

Reed: Have you made contact with any police agencies whatsoever trying to obtain work from them?

Ben: No.

Reed: Now, from September of 1991 until March of 1992, did you maintain any kind of telephone contact with the Doctor?

Ben: No.

Reed: May I check my notes, your Honor?

The Court: Yes.

Reed: Now, in September, in working for the FBI, you knew at that point in time that you were an informant; true?

Ben: Yes.

Reed: And you knew that when you were interacting with the Doctor in September of 1991, that you were working with the FBI; right?

Ben: Yes.

Reed: And you knew that you were, in talking with the Doctor, lying to the Doctor with respect to what your intentions were concerning the drug trade; correct?

Ben: Yes.

Reed: And during the course of the first meeting that you had with the Doctor, you lied to him during that meeting; right?

Ben: Yes.

Reed: And lied to Paul?

Ben: Yes.

Reed: And all throughout the other meetings that you had with the Doctor since September, you were lying to him then; correct?

43

Ben: Yes.

Reed: And had you worked on any other undercover – without telling me which ones, had you worked on any other undercover operations with the FBI up till September of 1991?

Ben: I was working on one. Yes.

Reed: And you made contact with drug dealers?

Ben: Yes.

Reed: And you were lying to these other drug dealers in the course of being an informant with the FBI in these other cases; right?

Ben: Yes.

Reed: And in order for you in your mind to continue to be paid by the FBI, you knew that it was important for you to be a convincing liar; correct?

Ben: No.

Reed: In coming into contact with the Doctor you wanted to be paid by the FBI; correct?

Ben: Yes.

Reed: You knew that obviously in your mind that if the Doctor thought that you were working in an undercover capacity, that this might cause you some problem; right?

Ben: No.

Reed: In your mind, did you think that you would have to be a good liar in order to be an undercover informant?

Ben: A good liar. No.

Reed: In your mind, did you think you had to be a convincing liar?

Ben: Perhaps.

44

Reed: Now, during the course of the last year—what I mean by that is 1992 up to the current—up until you stopped working with the FBI, you were working in other investigations with them; right?

Ben: Yes.

Reed: Without telling me the nature of those investigations, you came into contact with many people that you lied to; would that be fair to say?

Ben: Yes.

Reed: Did you enjoy your line of work with the FBI?

Ben: No.

Reed: Did you believe you were a convincing liar?

Ben: I don't know.

Reed: Now, did the FBI indicate to you, words to the effect that you were going to receive any kind of payment, a witness fee, for example, for coming to court today?

Ben: They were going to pay my expenses, yes.

Reed: And did you have to fly in from someplace to come to court today?

Ben: Yes.

Reed: Did they indicate to you that they would give you some extra money besides the expenses?

Ben: I talked to somebody. I think that it was to the tune of something like $40 a day.

Reed: And you are staying at the present time at a hotel wherein the expenses are paid?

Ben: Yes.

Reed: Did you ever take any photographs whatsoever of the sailboat that's depicted in Exhibit 1?

Ben: No.

Reed: Did you ever take any kind of photographs of the interior of the boat?

Ben: No.

Reed: I have no further questions, your honor.

The Court: All right. Mark.

Mark: No further questions, your honor.

The Court: All right. You may step down.

Mark: The government calls as its next witness, agent FBI agent Tim.

Agent Tim is sworn in:

The Clerk: You may be seated agent Tim.

Mark: What is your occupation?

Tim: I'm a special agent with the FBI.

Mark: How long have you worked with the FBI?

Tim: Six and a half years.

Mark: What is your present assignment?

Tim: I'm assigned to work drug investigations for the Los Angeles division.

Mark: How long have you been assigned to work drug investigations in Los Angeles?

Tim: Since October first 1991.

Mark: In your capacity as a special agent working drug investigations, were you involved in the surveillance or monitoring of a sailboat called the Driven?

Tim: Yes.

Mark: When did that begin?

Tim: October 1991.

Mark: What was your role?

46

Tim: I received periodic reports from personnel assigned to joint task force 5 in Oakland, California, as to the location of the sailboat Driven.

Mark: Over what period of time was the Driven monitored?

Tim: October 1991 through March of 1992.

Mark: Do you know if the sailboat had been monitored prior to the time that you arrived in Los Angeles?

Tim: Yes.

Mark: Had it been?

Tim: Yes.

Mark: In October of 1991, when you began working in Los Angeles, where was the Driven located?

Tim: Long Beach.

Mark: To your knowledge, did the Driven leave Long Beach, at any point after that?

Tim: Yes.

Mark: When?

Tim: Middle of December.

Reed: Objection, your honor, Calls for hearsay.

The Court: I think you have answered the question.

Mark: Special Agent, do you know where the Driven went in December 1991?

Reed: Objection. No foundation.

The Court: Well, he can answer yes or no. And let's find out if there is a foundation so he can tell us.

Mark: Yes, your honor.

The Court: All right. What is your answer?

Tim: Yes.

Mark: Where did it go?

The Court: Well, now you have to lay the foundation.

Mark: How did you learn where the Driven went in December 1991?

Tim: I received a report from joint task force 5.

Reed: I rest my case, your honor.

Mark: Did any personal—

Reed: There is no foundation.

Mark: Do you have any personal knowledge as to where the Driven went in December 1991?

The Court: You mean—

Mark: From personal observation.

The Court: Other than what he was told?

Mark: Yes.

Tim: Other than what I was told, no.

Mark: No further questions, your honor.

The Court: All right. Attorney Reed.

Reed: Agent Tim, to be clear, you didn't follow the sailboat in some kind of helicopter and watch where it went; right?

Tim: No.

Reed: With your own eyes; correct?

Tim: No.

Reed: Now, in October you didn't also drive down the coast of California and keep your eyes on this sailboat; correct?

Tim: Correct.

Reed: Now, in October of 1991, were you working with a person by the name of Ben C------r?

Tim: Yes.

Mark: Objection. Beyond the scope of direct, your honor.

The Court: It is beyond the scope of direct. It appears to me it is, anyway.

Reed: Very well.

Reed: Does the FBI have available to it cameras to investigate crimes?

Mark: Beyond the scope of direct.

The Court: Well, I suppose it is. Overruled.

Reed: I won't be very long in this area, your honor.

The Court: All right.

Reed: Does it have available to it cameras in the conducting of investigations?

Tim: Yes.

Reed: Does it have tape recorders in conducting investigations?

Tim: Yes.

Reed: In the Los Angeles office?

Tim: Yes.

Reed: Would it be fair to say the FBI throughout the United States has these tools?

Tim: Yes.

Reed: Does it have available wire transmitters?

Mark: Objection to this line of questioning as irrelevant, your honor.

The Court: Well—

Reed: A couple more and I'll be done.

The Court: All right. You may answer.

Tim: Could you clarify what you mean by wire transmitters?

Reed: Where a person is wearing in an undercover area of his body a transmitter so that the other person they are interacting with can hear conversations.

Tim: Yes.

Reed: That's commonly referred to as a wire; correct?

Tim: Yes.

Reed: No further questions.

Mark: No further questions.

The Court: You may step down.

Mark: Your honor, the government expects the next witness to take more than 15 minutes. Would you like me to begin with him?

The Court: Well, let's begin with him.

Mark: The government calls Coast Guard Boatswain Huey.

(Huey is sworn in)

Mark: What is your occupation?

Huey: I work for the U.S. Coast Guard.

Mark: How long?

Huey: six years.

Mark: What is your present assignment?

Huey: I'm assigned to the Tactical Law Enforcement Team in San Diego.

Mark: What does that entail?

Reed: Objection. Relevancy.

The Court: To this question?

Reed: Yes, your honor.

The Court: Your question was?

Mark: What type of laws is his unit responsible for enforcing?

The Court: Objection is overruled. You may answer.

Huey: We enforce any applicable laws.

Mark: Have you received any training in the detection of drug-related crimes?

Huey: Yes.

Mark: What type of training?

Huey: Two law enforcement schools.

Mark: How long have you been on the task force?

Huey: Two years.

Mark: Were you working on the tactical law enforcement team on March 23rd, 1992?

Huey: Yes.

Mark: Where were you working?

Huey: I was working on board the USS Vincennes. We were on patrol off the coast of Mexico.

The Court: Is that a Navy cruiser?

Huey: Yes.

Mark: Is the tactical law enforcement team of the Coast Guard often stationed aboard Navy Vessels?

Reed: Objection. Relevancy.

The Court: Overruled.

Huey: Yes. That's our primary platform we work off.

Mark: What was your mission on March 23rd, 1992?

Huey: To intercept and to board the sailboat Driven.

Mark: Did you locate the Driven?

Huey: Yes.

Mark: When?

Huey: The morning of March 23rd, 1992.

Mark: Approximately what time?

Huey: 1:30am.

Mark: I ask you to look at government's Exhibit 1. Do you recognize it?

Huey: Yes.

Mark: What is it?

Huey: A picture of the Driven.

Mark: Where did you locate the vessel?

Huey: 40 miles north of Cedros Island, which is off the Baja Peninsula, Mexico.

Mark: What was the vessels course?

Huey: Due North.

Mark: What happened then?

Huey: Lieutenant Gay, was my supervisor, he asked them routine---

Reed: Objection, your honor. Calls for hearsay.

The Court: I think you've answered the question.

Mark: What did Lieutenant Gay do after you located the Driven?

Huey: He asked them routine boarding questions.

Reed: Your honor, just to interpose an objection with respect to the use of the word 'them.'

Mark: Did you board the Driven?

The Court: Wait just a minute, please. I have to rule on that now.

Mark: I apologize, your honor.

The Court: Your objection is what again?

Reed: The Boatswain has and seems to be testifying in a manner where he is relating: We asked them, them, them. The word 'them' has a compound use, your honor. I think it gives an unfair—

The Court: All right. The answer will be stricken because it's ambiguous as to what he means by the word 'them.'

Mark: Huey, do you know how many people were on board the Driven on March 23rd, 1992, prior to your boarding?

Huey: Two people.

Mark: Did you board the Driven?

Huey: Yes.

Mark: By yourself?

The Court: Wait now. When you say, did you, are you talking about him individually?

Mark:

Reed: The Boatswain has and seems to be testifying in a manner where he is relating: We asked them, them, them. The word 'them' has a compound use, your honor. I think it gives an unfair—

The Court: All right. The answer will be stricken because it's ambiguous as to what he means by the word 'them.'

Mark: Huey, do you know how many people were on board the Driven on March 23rd, 1992, prior to your boarding?

Huey: Two people.

Mar: Did you board the Driven?

Huey: Yes.

Mark: By yourself?

The Court: Wait now. When you say, did you, are you talking about him individually?

Mark: Yes.

The Court: Or his team, or what?

Mark: Individually at first.

The Court: All right.

Huey: Not individually.

The Court: Personally?

Huey: Yes, personally.

Mark: Were you by yourself?

Huey: No.

Mark: Who else boarded the Driven with you?

Huey: Dewy and Louie.

Mark: At what time?

Huey: 3:00am.

Mark: Did you personally speak to anyone on board the Driven?

Huey: Yes.

Mark: Who was that?

Huey: I asked who the master was? Or who was in charge of the vessel. He identified himself as Paul.

Mark: You mentioned that there were two people on board. Who else was on board?

Huey: The Doctor.

Mark: Do you see him in the courtroom today?

Huey: Yes.

Mark: Could you point at him, and tell us what he is wearing?

Huey: Sitting there in the multi colored shirt.

Mark: I would like the record to state that the witness has pointed at the Doctor.

The Court: The record will so reflect.

Mark: What did you say to the Captain, Paul, after you boarded?

Huey: I explained that the Coast Guard was on board today to insure that he was in compliance with any and all applicable U.S. law; or something to that effect. I was in charge you know.

Mark: What was it that you intended to do?

Huey: To enforce any applicable U.S. laws that I saw fit. I was in charge you know.

Mark: How did you intend to go about that?

Huey: I begin the process of Coast Guard boarding by conducting my initial safety inspection.

Mark: What is an initial safety inspection?

Huey: To insure there are no safety hazards on board.

Mark: Did you and your boarding party conduct such an inspection?

Huey: Yes I did, I mean we did I guess.

Mark: What did you do when you finished?

Huey: Paul and Myself went over the paperwork of a 4100 form?

Reed: Objection. Relevancy.

The Court: Overruled.

Reed: Also calls for hearsay.

The Court: Overruled.

Huey: A standard safety form.

Mark: In the course of filling out the 4100 form, did you ask Paul what nationality the boat was?

Reed: Objection, your honor, calls for hearsay from this other person who is not on trial.

The Court: All right. Let's determine where the defendant was at the time.

Mark: May I approach?

The Court: Yes, you mean side bar?

Mark: Yes.

The Court: All right. Bring the stenographer with you.

(SIDE BAR CONFERENCE OUTSIDE THE HEARING OF THE JURY)

Mark: Your honor, with respect to the statements of Paul, particularly during the boarding. It's the government's—

The Court: Well, is there a conspiracy charged?

Mark: No, but, your honor, it's the government's position that even without a charge of conspiracy, the statements are admissible as statements in furtherance of a common scheme or plan.

Reed: This is kind of an easy analysis, your honor, I think, because there is no furtherance of the conspiracy. The

Coast Guard was on the boat. They were asking the person about registration of the boat. That has nothing to do with statements made by a coconspirator to carry out his drug activities. He is responding to the Coast Guard concerning things. It's not in furtherance of anything.

The Court: Well, if the Doctor was present and these—and this conversation was taking place, then I can see that there is no particular problem there. But you cannot lay that foundation.

Mark: I'm not sure the Doctor was even present, your honor. But it's the government's position that any statements made to law enforcement, or in this case the Coast Guard, while they were investigating the Driven were in furtherance of the conspiracy, and the statements would go to—

The Court: You know, I understand that. But there is no conspiracy charged. No conspiracy charge. Now, how do we make the jump from the fact that there is no conspiracy charged in this case? How do we get coconspirators and use all the rules that relate to conspiracy in a case where there is no conspiracy charged. That's why I'm troubled.

Mark: It's the government's position that a conspiracy need not be charged.

The Court: Do you have authority for that?

Mark: Perhaps I could brief that. I'll stay away from that area until the end of the day.

The Court: All right. You let me know what authority there is, and we'll look at it.

Mark: I will, your honor.

(WITHIN HEARING OF THE JURY)

Mark: Huey, prior to boarding the Driven, did you notice anything that indicated that the vessel was registered?

Huey: Yes.

Mark: What was that?

Huey: In the forward part of the boat, on the left side, were what we refer to as C.F. numbers, because the first two digits are CF, which indicate that it's registered in the state of California.

The Court: You mean on the bow?

Huey: Yes.

The Court: On the hull.

Huey: Yes.

Mark: Your honor, I would ask at this point the clerk place before the witness government's Exhibit 2 for identification.

(Exhibit placed)

Mark: Huey, do you recognize government's Exhibit 2?

Huey: Yes.

Mark: What is it?

Huey: It is a picture of the CF numbers on the sailing vessel Driven.

Mark: Does government's Exhibit 2 fairly and accurately depict that portion of the Driven as it appeared on March 23rd, 1992?

Huey: Yes.

Mark: Your honor, at this point we would move government's Exhibit 2 into evidence.

The Court: Received.

Mark: Huey, what is it about government's exhibit— or the symbols and letters depicted in Exhibit 2 that indicates to you that the vessel was registered at the time of boarding?

Huey: The red sticker to the right indicates the sticker was given to the registered owner. That it is legally registered in the State of California.

Mark: Huey, you testified that you completed the paperwork aspect of the inspection. What is involved?

Huey: We write down vessel information. There is a whole list of things on the 4100 form. I know most of them. I was in charge of the inspection, you know.

Mark: Right, okay. Did you conduct a form 4100 inspection?

Huey: Yes, I did, I mean we.

Mark: Did you notice anything unusual?

Huey: Yes.

Mark: What was that?

Huey: Is this trial going to be made into a movie?

The Court: All right. I think this is the time we'll take our adjournment.

Mark: Thank you, your honor.

The Court: You may step down, Boatswain.

As I indicated ladies and gentlemen, tomorrow is a legal holiday. We'll not be in session. We'll resume on Thursday at 9:00am. Remember the admonition of the court. You are excused until Thursday, 9:00am.

(PROCEEDINGS ADJOURNED)

Reed and I talked while I was being handcuffed. The others in the courtroom gathered their papers, brief cases, and assorted desk clutter. Reed was doing well. The jurors would nod at me, give me an occasional smile, or stare. I was exhausted. Deeply exhausted and stressed at the testimony, and time involved in this little bust.

I was escorted down to the holding cell in the basement of the courthouse. I was alone. The time was almost four in the afternoon. I sat alone, in the cold, steel benched holding cell. I looked at some of the graffiti scratched into the many coats of beige paint.

By six o'clock I was escorted into a Marshal's van, and brought over to MDC. I was given a hangar for my clothes, and issued a new jumpsuit. The elevator dropped me on the ninth floor. I was now home again from a hard days work.

Immediately the few people I talked to on the floor came up to me and asked how the court went. We talked, played cribbage, and I fit in a game of chess before ten o'clock lock down.

I called Meg the next day and kept her up to date on the proceedings. Meg was tired too, so was my family, and friends. They knew, as well as I did, that if I was found guilty, ten years would be the minimum. I reflected on my past business for the first time ever. I never knew how much I had hurt my family and friends. I was gone, out of site, but not out of their minds. This is the part of the drug, or any crime game a person must learn to deal with. This is the hardest part of the game. The party is over, but life goes on. At least in my mind, I knew I had done this to myself. I should have been sharp enough to know that Ben was and is a Rat. I should have seen the signs. But, life goes on. I now must deal with the situation at hand. Plus, my cribbage game sucked lately, I couldn't concentrate. I got beat in chess by a guy who opened with a Queen's Gambit. I knew the Gambit from the first move, and didn't see it coming.

Holiday's in the joint are the worst. There is no mail call, you can feel the holiday, but you cannot participate. Prison is just another day, after day. I was happy to have Veteran's Day behind us. I had trial in the morning.

(LOS ANGELES, CALIFORNIA; THURSDAY, NOVEMBER 12, 1992; 9:00 AM)

(OUTSIDE THE PRESENCE OF THE JURY)

Mark: Good morning, your honor.

Reed: Good morning, your honor. The Doctor is not here yet.

The Court: I realize that, but we have a problem with a juror. She has some kind of a problem. Something about an illness in the family. We can bring her in and question her about it, if that is suitable to you.

Reed: It is, your honor.

Mark: Yes, your honor.

The Court: Is there any reason for the Doctor to be here for that?

Reed: No.

Mark: No.

The Court: Summon her in.

The Court: What we'll do is this, after I interrogate her, then I'll ask you to come to the side bar and see whether or not we should further inquire or excuse her, or just what.

Mark: Very well.

(WITHIN THE PRESENCE OF JUROR NUMBER 11)

The Court: How are you?

Juror: Fine.

The Court: My clerk advises me that you told her of some problem that has occurred in your family.

Juror: Yes.

The Court: What is it?

Juror: My grandma's heart is failing.

The Court: Your grandma what?

Juror: Her heart is failing.

The Court: Her heart is failing?

Juror: Yes. We are not expecting her to live. I just lost my mom five months ago.

The Court: Is she here locally?

Juror: No.

The Court: Where does she live?

Juror: Texas.

The Court: Texas?

Juror: Uh-huh.

The Court: So what is your intent?

Juror: To go to Texas.

The Court: Well, gentlemen, do you have any questions? Do you want a side bar?

Reed: I would like to thank the juror, and wish her well. Please excuse her.

Mark: I have no objection, I guess.

The Court: You are excused juror.

Reed: Your honor, while we are waiting, would it be advisable at this point for me to file some jury instructions that I thought would be appropriate?

The Court: Oh, yes.

Mark: I will file too.

The Court: Remember this is off the record.

(DISCUSSION OFF THE RECORD)

The Court: We are ready to have the jury brought in.

(WITHIN THE PRESENCE OF THE JURY)

The Court: Good morning, ladies and gentlemen.

The Court: One of our jurors has a serious illness in her family and has been excused. So that means the alternate juror. So, take her seat please, and you are now a juror.

Mark: The government recalls Boatswain Huey.

The Court: All right.

The Clerk: I would remind you that you are still under oath.

Mark: During the boarding of the Driven, did the defendant provide you with any identification?

Huey: Yes.

Mark: What was it?

Huey: A passport.

Mark: A United States passport?

Huey: Yes.

Mark: During your inspection of the Driven, did you notice anything unusual?

Huey: Yes.

Mark: What did you notice?

Huey: We found fiberglass, and woodworking that didn't seem normal to me.

Mark: What was that?

Huey: The screws seemed new and shiny to me.

Mark: Did you ask the Doctor about that area of the boat?

Huey: Yes.

Mark: What did you ask him?

Huey: I asked him if there had ever been any woodwork on board to his knowledge. He said he didn't know of any. It was not his boat.

Mark: How did the Doctor act when you searched the aft of the boat?

Reed: Objection. Calls for a conclusion, also no foundation.

The Court: Sustained in that form.

Mark: Did you ask Paul about any work being done?

Reed: Objection. Asked and answered a second ago.

Mark: I'm referring to Paul.

The Court: I think he is on a second person.

Reed: Yes.

Huey: Yes I did.

Mark: What did Paul say?

Reed: Objection. Hearsay.

Mark: I'm not offering it for the truth. Just for the effect on Huey.

The Court: You are offering it for what?

Mark: The effect it had on Huey.

The Court: The effect it had on him is irrelevant. Sustained.

Mark: After asking the Doctor whether any woodwork had been done, what did you do next?

Huey: I continued the boarding.

Mark: What did you do after that?

Huey: I called Lieutenant Gay to tell him I had found shiny screws in the woodwork. Lieutenant Gay told me to gain access behind the shiny screws. I was in charge, you know.

Mark: And did you remove the woodwork?

Huey: I told Dewey to do it.

Mark: Did Dewey do it?

Huey: Yes, I was in charge.

Mark: What happened when he removed the trim?

Huey: A white fiberglass panel that matched the rest of the boat fell away. It is unusual for boats to have work done on them. Some openings were exposed too.

Mark: Were the openings covered?

Huey: Yes.

Mark: How were they covered?

Huey: With a separate piece of fiberglass.

Mark: What was behind the cover?

Huey: Several clear plastic packages.

Mark: Approximately how many packages?

Huey: The first compartment contained 30 packages.

Mark: Your honor, at this point I would ask permission to have special agent Weed approach the witness stand with government's Exhibit 5 for identification.

The Court: Very well.

Mark: Does government's Exhibit 5 resemble the packages you found?

Huey: Yes.

Mark: After locating the packages, what did you do next?

Huey: I instructed Dewey and Louie to secure the area. I handcuffed them. I conducted several field tests.

These tests I use a spray test with two sprays. You rub the product on the test paper, then spray can 1, then can 2, and if you get a red color, it is positive for THC.

Mark: What is THC?

Huey: An element found in marijuana.

Mark: What did the tests you performed indicate?

Huey: That it was marijuana in the packages.

Mark: What did you do then after the positive test?

Huey: I contacted Lieutenant Gay, told him I had a positive field test for marijuana. He instructed me to arrest the individuals, and seize the boat.

Mark: After arresting them, what did you do?

Huey: Informed them that they were under arrest for violating U.S. Laws, and prepared them for transport back to the USS Vincennes.

Mark: After they were transported back to the USS Vincennes, what did you do next?

Huey: I gained access to six more hidden compartments.

Mark: And were the six compartments similar to the first compartment?

Huey: Yes.

Mark: Did you find anything in those compartments?

Huey: Yes, we found a total of 103 packages of marijuana.

Mark: What did you do with the packages?

Huey: I transported them back to the ship.

Mark: What did you do with them on board?

Huey: Locked them in a vault. I had the key.

Mark: No further questions, your honor.

The Court: Reed for cross-examination.

CROSS EXAMINATION

Reed: On March 23rd, 1992, you on board the USS Vincennes; correct?

Huey: Yes.

Reed: And when you were on board that ship, did you see this sailboat off in the distance?

Huey: Yes.

Reed: What time of night was that?

Huey: Sometime after 1:00 am.

Reed: Would it be fair to say that it was dark?

Huey: Yes, very dark.

Reed: And it's true that you had not seen the Driven before that particular sighting; correct?

Huey: Yes.

Reed: You had not seen where the Driven had come from; right?

Huey: Not visually with my eyes.

Reed: You had not seen—now when you saw the Driven off in the distance, the Vincennes was how far away?

Huey: I couldn't even—I mean I couldn't guess how far.

Reed: Had you by chance, tracked the Driven on some kind of radar?

Huey: Yes.

Reed: So there was radar contact before you saw it?

Huey: Yes.

Reed: When your party departed the Vincennes, it traveled towards the Driven; true?

Huey: Yes.

Reed: And you went in a smaller boat over to the Driven; correct?

Huey: Correct.

Reed: And when you got to the Driven, did you notice whether or not the Driven was on autopilot?

Huey: At some point it was on autopilot.

Reed: Paul was on deck; correct?

Huey: Yes.

Reed: You can't tell if you saw Paul or the Doctor first on deck; correct?

Huey: I cannot remember.

Reed: What is an autopilot?

Huey: An electronic or wind driven machine that steers the boat.

Reed: And with an autopilot that means that somebody doesn't have to actually steer the boat; right?

Huey: yes.

Reed: This machinery called an autopilot does it automatically; correct?

Huey: Yes.

Reed: Now, after boarding the boat, you determined that the Doctor was the sole passenger on the boat; correct?

Huey: Yes, the Doctor was identified as the sole passenger, and Paul the Master and owner of the boat.

Reed: You did not see for example the Doctor fixing the sails on deck as you approached; correct?

Huey: No.

Reed: Was the Doctor steering the boat in any way?

Huey: No.

Reed: So it is fair to say that the Doctor was not seen doing any chores such as fixing sails, anchoring, checking the sheets, anything of this nature?

Huey: No.

Reed: And after boarding the boat you determined Paul was in charge of the boat?

Huey: Yes.

Reed: He told you that; right?

Huey: Yes.

Reed: And he is the master of the boat; correct?

Huey: Yes.

Reed: With the court's permission, may I approach the Mark for a second?

The Court: Yes.

(DISCUSSION OFF THE RECORD BETWEEN COUNSELS)

Reed: Your honor, with the court's permission, I would like to have marked next in order, or whichever way you would like, our Exhibit to be marked. We're only going to have one exhibit, your honor.

The Court: Well, we'll mark it by letter the, Defendant's 'A.'

Reed: Very well. I'll put an 'A' on the back of the document. May I approach the witness, your honor?

The Court: You may.

Reed: Huey, you determined that the registration of this boat was for Paul; correct?

Huey: Yes.

Reed: And you explained to us when you were being asked questions by the Assistant United States Attorney how Coast Guard personnel can tell whether or not a boat is registered in the U.S.

Huey: The most important one is the registration that the Master has to, by law, have onboard. It has to be the original copy sent to him from the state. And from there, it has all types of information like the hull identification number to the C.F. numbers assigned, which should be on the bow.

Reed: Paul produced the original registration for?

Huey: Yes.

Reed: And does that document that's before you, Defense 'A' accurately reflect the registration of this vessel?

Huey: What it looked like to me is a—like a DMV—this is not exactly what your registration should look like. This is the same information, but it's on a, like a DMV interdepartmental type format.

Reed: And the vessels are registered with the DMV; correct?

Huey: In the State of California they are. Yes.

Reed: Is there anything that's on that document which is inconsistent with the numbers that were shown to you by, Paul?

Huey: I couldn't tell you that without looking at all the 4100 form, comparing them. And I don't know that this is the same information that was on the actual registration form I saw that day.

Reed: The registration form you saw that day reflected that the boat was not registered to the Doctor; correct?

Huey: That is correct.

Reed: Just to Paul, the owner and Captain?

Huey: Yes.

Reed: Now, from the point in time that you boarded the vessel until the point in time that you left, the two individuals who were on the boat, the Doctor, and Paul, were being watched by the Coast Guard personnel; correct?

Huey: Yes.

Reed: And there came a point in time when you—and the boat was sailing, the Driven was still sailing as the two individuals were being watched by Coast Guard personnel; correct?

Huey: Yes, the boat was under power or sail.

Reed: And that's because if you don't allow it to be under power, the waves could rock the boat severely; right?

Huey: In the right weather, yes.

Reed: Was there a storm going on during this period?

Huey: No. There was a rainsquall, but only 3 to 5 foot seas.

Reed: Now, the people in charge of seeing that the boat maintained its power and course were Coast Guard personnel as your duties were taking place; correct?

Huey: No.

Reed: Now, when you started to search the boat, you went down—did you ever go down below into the mess deck area?

Huey: Immediately upon boarding, and when I had paperwork to do I went below.

Reed: Now, there came a point in time when you went below deck; right?

Huey: Yes.

71

Reed: And approximately how much time did you spend down below deck before the point in time when this compartment was located?

Huey: An hour and a half, at least that long, I can't even tell you how many times I went below deck.

Reed: Now, the point at which you noticed the smell of marijuana was after that sealed compartment was opened; correct?

Huey: Yes.

Reed: And you had been going back and forth top deck, below deck, several times before you noticed that smell of the marijuana; correct?

Huey: Yes.

Reed: And that occurred after the compartment was opened; correct?

Huey: Yes.

Reed: After the packages of marijuana were found, did you take custody of them?

Huey: Yes.

Reed: Were you the person who was responsible for taking custody of the marijuana packages?

Huey: Yes. From the moment the two individuals were arrested to the moment that it was turned over to U.S. Customs agents I was responsible, I was in charge, I was the custodian of the packages, I watched them closely.

Reed: Now, after you obtained the marijuana packages, you took them back to the Vincennes; right?

Huey: Yes, I was in charge.

Reed: Ok, and you placed them in some kind of locked vault; true?

Huey: Yes.

Reed: And they remained there; right?

Huey: Yes.

Reed: And released over to U.S. Customs?

Huey: Yes.

Reed: From the point in time that you came into custody of the numerous packages that are displayed—I don't recall the number of the Exhibit, but the exhibit that's up there on the board—from the point in time that you had custody of the packages, did you ever do what's called fingerprint dusting of the packages?

Huey: No, I did not. That's not Coast Guard boarding procedure. That is—

Reed: I'm just asking a simple question.

Huey: No, uh, I did not.

Reed: You didn't do it; right?

Huey: No.

Reed: When you handed them to the U.S. Customs agent at the Naval Shipyard, did you see him take custody of the packages?

Huey: Yes.

Reed: Now, you don't remember the name of the person, but you knew that he was a Customs official; correct?

Huey: He presented identification.

Reed: Did you do any—attempt to do any fingerprint dusting of the areas around the secret compartments that were located on this vessel?

Huey: No.

Reed: Did you see any other individuals who were in your team conduct any kind of fingerprint dusting within the interior of the compartments on the Driven?

Huey: No, they did not.

Reed: Did you have that ordered after the Driven was eventually returned to Long Beach?

Huey: No, but I was in charge.

Reed: Your honor, with the court's permission may I take a look at the packaging on one of these kilos? I think one was produced in court.

The Court: Yes.

Reed: May I approach the witness?

The Court: All right.

(REED SHOWING PACKAGE TO WITNESS)

Reed: Would it be fair to say that this is a fair representation of the packaging on all the numerous bundles that you did find on the Driven, on March 23rd, 1992?

Huey: Yes.

Reed: Same type of surface covering?

Huey: Yes.

Reed: There is one that we can see here in Exhibit number 7 that appears not to have as much duct tape but has plastic wrapping around it; right?

Huey: Yes.

Reed: And I'm pointing to the third row over from the right, about three packages down; correct?

Huey: Yes.

Reed: I have no further questions, your honor.

Mark: Just a couple of questions.

(REDIRECT EXAMINATION)

Mark: Huey, was the Doctor steering the Driven at any point during the boarding?

Huey: Yes.

Mark: For approximately what period of time?

Huey: I couldn't give a time. I could say that the majority of the time I spent directly with the master of the vessel, Paul. The Doctor, whether he was steering the rudder manually or if he was just up there paying attention because, as I said, different things affect autopilot. He was up at the helm area for the majority of the boarding in the general vicinity of the tiller. How often he had to adjust it, I don't remember.

Mark: During the boarding did you ask the defendant any questions about the boat?

Huey: Yes.

Mark: What type of questions did you ask him?

Huey: As I stated earlier, I had asked him if he knew of any woodwork being done on the boat.

Reed: Objection, your honor, this is asked and answered.

The Court: Well, it has been asked and answered. Are you going after something different?

Mark: Did you have any discussions with him about the boat other than the discussions you testified to?

Huey: Yes.

Mark: What was the nature of those discussions?

Huey: I had asked him if, what type of voyage they had been on.

Mark: Did he respond to your question?

Huey: Yes.

Mark: What type of voyage had they been on?

Huey: A pleasure voyage. They had been gone—

Reed: Objection. Calls for a conclusion.

The Court: He is just asking what he said.

Huey: I understand.

Mark: Did he tell you he had left on the Driven from Los Angeles?

Huey: I don't remember that.

Mark: Did he tell you how long he had been on the Driven?

Huey: I remember something to the effect of the entire voyage.

Mark: Did they—

Huey: With the exception of Paul flying once in awhile to the States, which he told me he had done.

Mark: Did the Doctor tell you how long he had been on the Driven, approximately?

Huey: I can't say how long.

Mark: You testified on cross-examination that the passengers were being watched by Coast Guard personnel during the entire boarding; is that right?

Huey: Yes.

Mark: Does that include the defendant and Paul?

Huey: Yes.

(RECROSS-EXAMINATION)

Reed: Huey, while Paul was taken down below, it was during those periods of time that you saw the Doctor at the helm; right?

Huey: He was by the helm at that point and when I would come back on deck.

Reed: And so I take it, Coast Guard personnel weren't at that point—while Paul was below deck, Coast

76

Guard personnel were not in any way touching the wheel of the boat; right?

Huey: Correct.

Reed: Is this the type of boat that had a wheel or the type of boat that had one of those sticks?

The Court: A tiller.

Reed: A tiller?

Huey: It was a tiller.

Reed: And you can't recall whether or not you ever saw the Doctor touch the tiller during those periods of time that Paul was taken below deck; right?

Huey: He was sitting no more than inches away from it. I can't say that I saw him adjusting it. There were times when the sailboat and the Vincennes would come close together, and, you know, at different intervals.

Reed: And it was at those periods of time that you felt that the Doctor was steering the vessel that Paul was below deck; right?

Huey: At almost anytime I could turn around and see who was sitting and minding the helm at the time.

Reed: And you said that it is important for this boat to remain on course so that it doesn't get knocked around in the seas as you were searching on this evening; right?

Huey: I tell individuals to stay on their present course.

Reed: So you ordered the individuals to do this?

Huey: It was a blanket statement.

Reed: So it was a blanket statement you made?

Huey: It's a general statement.

Reed: It was only after that statement that you saw the Doctor up in this area of the helm; right?

Huey: I remember when the boat was first illuminated, when we first came aboard, on the scene to it, where I could visually see it, someone was at the helm. Whether they were steering it or if they were just sitting there watching the autopilot, I don't know. And I can't remember which of the individuals it was.

Reed: All I'm asking is the following simple question: When you boarded the boat, you gave a blanket statement to these two individuals to the effect to stay on course; right?

Huey: Yes.

Reed: And it was after that statement was made that you had seen the Doctor up in the tiller area that Paul was below deck; right?

Huey: Correct.

Reed: And it was only during those times that you saw him up in the tiller area; right?

Huey: There were times when Paul and the Doctor would be up on the weather deck in the same general area.

Reed: And the Coast Guard personnel were not responsible for keeping the boat on course after you gave the blanket statement; right?

Huey: While I'm on board this vessel, I have to assume all responsibility. I was in charge. You know, unless the master can't steer the vessel.

Reed: Yes, ok, now, during the course of the boat traveling in its—in its direction, you seem to recall that the boat was on autopilot most of the time; right?

Huey: I can't say most of the time; I just know that it was on autopilot at certain times. I cannot recall whether his hand, or their hands, whoever was on it. I can't remember that, but I was in charge. 90% of the time someone was sitting next to the tiller.

Reed: Objection, your honor, with respect to the last portion of the answer, the 90% part of the boarding be stricken.

Mark: The witness was testifying.

The Court: I'm not sure. Let's hear what he said. Read it back please.

(READ BACK)

The Court: All right. You may finish your answer.

Huey: 90% of the time of that boarding on the Driven, someone was sitting next to the tiller.

Reed: And that 90% of the time was after you had given the blanket statement to these individuals to steer the boat in a certain direction?

Huey: Yes, I was in charge.

Reed: Thank you. I have no further questions.

The Court: All right. I just need to ask a couple of questions for background.

The Court: The Vincennes is a very large ship isn't it?

Huey: Yes.

The Court: How did you get from the Vincennes to the Driven?

Huey: A small inflatable boat.

The Court: The means you illuminated the Driven was from the Vincennes signal tower?

Huey: Yes.

The Court: You were on watch at that time?

Huey: Yes.

The Court: How close did the Vincennes get to the Driven?

Huey: 300 yards.

The Court: Okay, I have no further questions.

Huey: Is this going to be made into a Hollywood movie?

Mark: Nothing further your honor.

Reed: Uh, no, your honor.

The Court: You may step down. You are excused.

Mark: Your honor, the government calls agent Hater.

The Court: All right.

(DIRECT EXAMINATION)

Mark: Agent Hater, by whom are you employed?

Hater: U.S. Customs Service.

Mark: What do you do?

Hater: I'm a special agent in charge.

Mark: For how long?

Hater: Five years.

Mark: What are your responsibilities?

Hater: We conduct all investigations pertaining to violations of U.S. Customs Laws.

Mark: Were you working on March 25th, 1992?

Hater: Yes.

Mark: Did you have occasion to meet the Doctor on that day?

Hater: Yes.

Mark: Where?

Hater: Long Beach Naval Station.

Mark: Why were you there?

Hater: I was assigned case agent of this investigation, and my particular duties for that day were to transport the defendants.

Mark: Did you transport the Doctor to jail that day?

Hater: Yes, it was me.

Reed: Objection. Relevancy.

Mark: I'll withdraw the question.

Mark: Did you take custody of certain evidence that day?

Hater: Yes, I did. Me.

Mark: Your honor, I would like the clerk to place Exhibit 4 before the witness.

(Exhibit placed)

Mark: Hater, do recognize this Exhibit?

Hater: Yes, I do.

Mark: What is it?

Hater: It is a passport.

Mark: Did you take custody of this?

Hater: If I could look inside to see the picture for sure.

Mark: Well?

Hater: Yes.

Mark: whose passport is this?

Hater: It is the Doctor's.

Mark: Your honor I move Exhibit 4 into evidence.

The Court: Received.

Mark: Have you seen the packages depicted in this photo before?

Hater: Yes.

Mark: When was the first time?

Hater: March 25th, 1992.

Mark: At the same time that you took custody of government's Exhibit 4 and the other evidence?

Hater: Yes.

Mark: Were you present when it was taken off the Vincennes?

Hater: Yes.

Mark: Did you take custody of the packages depicted in Exhibit 7?

Hater: No.

Mark: Who did?

Hater: Yes. My supervisor, but I was in charge.

Mark: Did you later see the packages?

Hater: Yes.

Mark: Where at?

Hater: The Customs House.

Mark: When was that?

Hater: April 7th, 1992.

Mark: Why were you at the Customs House?

Hater: To pick up a few packages for testing.

Mark: Did you pick up the samples?

Hater: Yes.

Mark: How many packages did you pick up?

Hater: Nine.

Mark: Did you transport them to the Venture County Sheriff's laboratory?

Hater: Yes.

Mark: Where are the remaining 94 packages that are depicted in government's Exhibit 7?

Hater: I guess in a vault at the Customs House. I don't know for sure.

Mark: How many pounds of marijuana were there?

Hater: 410 pounds.

Mark: No further questions.

The Court: Reed for cross-examination.

(CROSS-EXAMINATION)

Reed: Agent Hater, does the U.S. Customs Service have the ability to do fingerprint testing?

Hater: Not that I'm aware of.

Reed: And so it is fair to say that in this particular investigation, fingerprint testing has not been done on any of the packages that are depicted in the photograph?

Hater: No. None has been done.

Reed: Has any fingerprint testing been done within those compartments inside the Driven, to your knowledge?

Hater: No.

Reed: No further questions, your honor.

Mark: No further questions.

The Court: You may step down.

The Court: We will take our morning recess before you call your next witness. Fifteen minute recess.

(Recess is concluded)

Mark: The government calls Agent Limpwood.

(Limpwood sworn in)

Mark: Limpwood, by whom are you employed?

Limpwood: Currently employed as a special agent with the United States Customs Service, assigned to the Southern California Narcotic Task Force.

Mark: How long have you worked for the Customs Service?

Limpwood: 4 years.

Mark: For whom did you work before that?

Limpwood: I was a Special Agent for the Drug Enforcement Administration for 18 years.

Mark: What did you do for the DEA?

Limpwood: All facets of narcotic investigation, money laundering, narcotic investigation, undercover activity, methods of narcotic smuggling, narcotic dealing; just about everything to do with the narcotic business.

Mark: Where did you work prior to going to the DEA?

Limpwood: For the Customs Service and as a Police Officer.

Mark: What type of work were you doing for the Customs Service before you went to the DEA?

Limpwood: Narcotic smuggling, primarily narcotics being brought in from outside the U.S.

Mark: And as a Police Officer what type of work did you do?

Limpwood: Patrol and Vice.

Mark: What is your educational background?

Limpwood: I have a bachelors of science degree in public administration and a master in psychology.

Mark: Have you had any specialized education in the field of law enforcement?

Limpwood: Yes. I have 20 weeks training in narcotics laws.

Mark: Have you testified as an expert witness before in narcotic cases?

Limpwood: Yes.

Mark: How many times?

Limpwood: three hundred in state court, and fifty times in federal court.

Mark: Have you been involved in marijuana cases?

Limpwood: Yes.

Mark: How many cases?

Limpwood: two hundred.

Mark: Your honor, I have finished my foundational questions. Should I permit defense counsel to voir dire the witness at this time?

Reed: We don't wish to, your honor.

The Court: All right.

Mark: Are familiar with the street value of marijuana?

Limpwood: Yes.

Mark: Are familiar with the typical dosage units of marijuana?

Limpwood: Yes.

Mark: How is marijuana distributed to the end user?

Limpwood: By one gram amounts.

Mark: How much is an ounce of marijuana sold for?

Limpwood: five hundred dollars.

Mark: How is it packaged for large amounts?

Limpwood: One-pound packages.

Mark: How many ounces in a pound?

Limpwood: Uh, oh, I think sixteen.

Mark: How much is a pound of marijuana sold for?

Limpwood: Three thousand dollars.

Mark: How about in ounces?

Limpwood: I can't calculate that in my head.

Mark: No further questions.

The Court: Reed?

(CROSS-EXAMINATION)

Reed: Does the United States Customs Service have the ability to do fingerprint dusting of evidence?

Limpwood: Yes, of course.

Reed: No further questions.

The Court: You may be excused.

Limpwood: That is it?

The Court: You may step down.

(Jury recess)

(OUTSIDE THE PRESENCE OF THE JURY)

Reed: Your honor, I'm confident that the court is aware of that long line of cases within the ninth circuit that talk about passengers in automobiles, or people who are guests at residences, different hotel rooms, things of that nature.

The long line of cases—just some of them off the top of my head are the U.S. v Penagos case, the U.S. v Sanchez-Mata case; I don't have the cities with me, but I can get those, your honor—but the long line of cases that state that when there is a passenger in a vehicle or a guest in a residence, that that person does not exercise dominion and control over narcotics that may happen to be hidden within a vehicle, even if they know, for example, that narcotics are within a vehicle and they are driving in the car as a passenger—and there's various cases on point.

Even if they know that there is narcotics in the car and they're sitting as a passenger and the car is riding along the freeway, as a matter of law, they cannot be held accountable to be in violation of possession of narcotics for purposes of distribution for the simple fact that mere knowledge of existence of the drugs is not sufficient as a matter of law; there has to be what's called dominion and control over the narcotics.

Now, in this particular case, your honor, we know that the Vincennes came upon a boat out at sea. There has been really no testimony as to what occurred prior to the Vincennes approaching the 'Driven' in the nature of what occurred to load this boat with marijuana. There were no FBI agents or Mexican Federales brought into court to testify as to who loaded. There's no fingerprint evidence whatsoever as to who touched the kilos, no fingerprints around the secret compartments, et cetera, and no visualization by any of the crew on board the Vincennes that would indicate anything other than the fact that the Doctor really was a passenger in the boat.

Yet, when they got to the boat, there was an order that was given, a blanket statement given by Boatswain Huey, to the effect "make sure the boat is kept on course." And then after he gave that order, the Doctor was seen to be by the tiller. It's confusing as to whether or not he was steering the boat, adjusting the tiller, but it's neither here nor there because whatever he was doing at that point to keep the boat on course, it was in direct response to the order that was given.

In other words, what I'm trying to get at is, there has been no sightings of the Doctor being a crew member working on the boat, operating the sails, before the Vincennes saw him. So there's really no evidence in this case that he was nothing other than a passenger in the boat. And for that reason, your honor, we feel that he had no dominion or control over the marijuana. Even if he knew the marijuana was there, they haven't shown that dominion and control. And we would ask the case be dismissed.

Mark: Your honor, Ben C------r, testified that several months before the boat left Long Beach, the Doctor showed him the boat, told him that he and Paul owned the boat, showed him were hidden compartments were going to be, or had been, or were going to be installed to conceal drugs. He told Ben, that he intended to smuggle drugs from Mexico into the United States.

Huey, testified that he had several conversations with the Doctor concerning the boat. Specifically he testified to the fact that the Doctor told him that no work had been done on the boat, on repeated occasions. The Doctor was at the tiller of the boat for a substantial portion of the boarding. And from that, the jury could certainly infer that the Doctor had dominion and control over the boat.

There was also testimony from Huey that the defendant had been on the entire voyage with Paul. And for that reason, the government would object to the Rule 29 Motion and request it be denied.

The Court: Reed?

Reed: Submitted, your honor.

The Court: Well, I think Ben has given testimony that would dictate that the court should not grant this motion. Now, whether the jury believes his testimony or not is another story. But as the case stands now, that testimony is in the record, namely, that this defendant intended to smuggle; he was on the boat when the contraband was found; apparently, it was a long voyage. And I think at this point in time, we would have to describe him more than just a passenger. Informants do not lie in my courtroom. Motion denied.

Reed: Your honor, we are not going to be presenting any evidence. The Doctor isn't going to be taking the stand, and—

The Court: He's not going to testify?

Reed: No, he is not. So, basically the case is finished at this point. There is nothing left but argument to occur.

The Court: All right. Well, maybe we can bring the jury back—well, let me ask you this: Have you looked at one another's jury instructions to see whether or not there are any controversial ones that are going to take some time to work out?

Mark: Your honor, I've had just a few minutes to look at the instructions submitted by the defendant. I would like the lunch hour, if possible, to go through them and to have a few minutes after lunch to argue the few instructions that we disagree on.

Reed: I have looked at the government's instructions, and there's about five of them that I object to. Other than that they are standard.

The Court: Well, we might use a few minutes before 12 o'clock and then have you come back at 1:30 and we'll finish them up. So then I will excuse the jury until 2 o'clock and we'll, hopefully, be ready to argue at 2:00 then.

Reed: Very well.

Mark: Very well.

The Court: You reserve your right to opening statement as well? You're not going to make an opening statement?

Reed: No. We would simply indicate on the record that we rest, your honor.

(WITHIN THE PRESENCE OF THE JURY)

The Court: All right. The government has rested. Reed?

Reed: The defense rests as well.

The Court: Ladies and gentlemen, the court is going to have to spend a short period of time going over the jury instructions with counsel, and it would appear that we'll be excused at this time and we'll reconvene at 2:00 pm. Leave your notebooks right there in the chairs.

(NOON RECESS)

(LOS ANGELES, CALIFORNIA; THURSDAY, NOVEMBER 12, 1992; 2:00 PM)

(OUTSIDE THE PRESENCE OF THE JURY)

The Court: One housekeeping matter. Will counsel stipulate that Exhibit 5, the package of marijuana, can be maintained in the custody and control of the case agent?

Reed: So stipulated.

Mark: Yes.

The Court: All right. Before we bring the jury in, the record will reflect that we've had our discussion on jury instructions, and the court has indicated the instructions it intends to give.

And I think, Reed, you had some objections you wish to place on the record.

Reed: Yes. To begin with, we object to the giving of the instruction, which talks about the fact that it's not necessary, to show that there was an actual sale made in order to find a person guilty of possession for sale of narcotics. We feel that it is redundant, superfluous. This is obviously a possession case, has nothing to do with a sale case; and therefore, it's superfluous.

I'm vehemently opposed to the giving of any aiding and abetting instruction. This case was an indictment, which charged the defendant as a principal. It did not allege within the indictment that he was a conspirator, a schemer, or an aider and abettor. The theory of culpability with respect to the Doctor is based on being a principal to a substantive offense. And we object to the giving of an aiding and abetting instruction at this late date. Other than that, those complete the specific objections we have to the instructions.

The Court: All right. Mark?

Mark: I would only add to that that the aiding and abetting instruction was proposed by the government on the theory that aiding and abetting is implied in every indictment and it was posed as an alternative to the common-scheme-and-plan instruction which was originally submitted by the government.

The Court: And this is true even if it isn't charged in the indictment, according to your position?

Mark: That's the government's position.

The Court: Well, the cases that I have been directed to seem to support that proposition. So I do intend to give that instruction. And I think the law, as I have found it, would support that. Do you have any objections you wish to put on record?

Mark: None, your honor. If I can add to the previous issue, though, that while counsel has reserved his right to object to that instruction, I would like to make it clear for the record that we have agreed to modify the ninth circuit instruction on aiding and abetting to include language regarding mere presence, which was suggested by the defendant.

The Court: Over the objection of defense counsel, the court intends to give that instruction, but we are going to substitute some of the language about mere presence, as found in the ninth circuit model instruction, with language that the two of you have agreed on. But this is—it's to be noted that Reed is not waiving his fundamental argument that this instruction should not be given at all.

Reed: Thank you.

The Court: All right. Summon the jury. And by the way, I don't intend to comment to the jury on the evidence. So I will not give that instruction.

(WITHIN THE PRESENCE OF THE JURY)

The Court: Both sides have rested, ladies and gentlemen, we are now going to proceed with final argument. Keep in mind, as I advised you earlier, this is not evidence but what the attorney's believe the evidence has constituted and how it fits into the law that applies to the case.

(COUNSELS FINAL ARGUMENTS AND THE COURT'S JURY INSTRUCTIONS ARE NOT TRANSCRIBED HEREIN FOR THE PURPOSE OF A PARTIAL TRANSCRIPT)

"Trying to retrieve the final arguments and jury instructions from the government was impossible."

The Court: Ladies and gentlemen, the court will make available to you, if you wish, the instructions that have just been read to you. But you may now retire and commence your deliberations and, of course, take your notebooks with you. You are excused now.

(THE JURORS RETIRE TO DELIBERATE.)

(OUTSIDE THE PRESENCE OF THE JURY)

The Court: My clerk is going to read into the record those exhibits, which she knows to be evidence.

Mark: With respect to the indictment, it makes reference to Paul. Does the court intend to redact it or send it back as—

The Court: Well, I didn't read the indictment. It wasn't requested, and so I didn't read it. And I don't know, I didn't tell them that they could have a copy of it. If they ask for a copy, we'll have to redact it. But, I don't know if they even want the jury instructions. If they do, we'll have to prepare those. There are a couple in there that need to be worked on.

Mark: The court in its charge to the jury referred to the fact that the indictment charges a violation of section 1803 and described offense. I think that should be sufficient.

The Court: I think that should be sufficient. And they heard the indictment read at the beginning of the case. It's now 4:15 pm. I'll probably call the jury back at 5 o'clock and see if they want to deliberate today or whether they would rather come back in the morning. And so, if you—I know where you will be Mark. Reed, will you be in the building?

Reed: I'll be up in the public defenders panel room, and I'll leave the number with your clerk.

The Court: All right.

Mark: We'll be here at 5 o'clock.

The Court: Otherwise, if you will be here at 5 o'clock, then I'll put the jury in the box and make that inquiry of them. If they ask for a copy of the instructions, there is no need for you to be present. I'll just send them in.

Reed: Very well.

Mark: Fine.

The Court: I'll see you at five.

Mark: Thank you.

The Court: And the Marshal is going to have the Doctor here at five.

Marshal: Uh, yes, your honor, yes, ok.

(RECESS)

Los Angeles, California; Thursday, November 12, 1992; 5:00 pm.

(WITHIN THE PRESENCE OF THE JURY)

The Court: In view of the hour, ladies and gentlemen, I have had you brought back into the courtroom. We had to make some—Well, we had to get the jury instructions prepared to be copied so that you could have a copy of them for your deliberations. May I inquire as to whom your foreperson is?

Juror Carol: I'am.

The Court: That's Carol -----?

Juror Carol: That is correct.

The Court: All right. Carol, we do have the instructions for you now if you want them, but I thought perhaps I should inquire as to whether you want to deliberate further this evening or whether you would rather come back in the morning?

Juror Carol: I don't think we are ready to make a decision. I think we should come back in the morning.

The Court: All right. Does that seem to be the belief of the rest of you? All right. You can come either at 9:00 or 9:30 in the morning.

Juror Carol: 9:00 is fine.

The Court: All right. You have been in deliberation a short time and it would be improper of you to talk to anyone about the case or to let anyone talk to you about the case. When you return in the morning, do not discuss the case until everyone is together. So you'll be excused now, and resume at 9:00 am tomorrow.

(PROCEEDINGS ADJOURNED)

All I wanted to do was get back to MDC. I was exhausted from just sitting back, and watching my life being dealt with by total strangers. My future was now in the hands of twelve people. Strangers, people who didn't even know each other.

Back at MDC dinner had been served. The men were watching tv, playing card games, ping pong, and lifting weights. The few men I knew asked me how the day went. I got in line for a phone. I called Meg, and my parents. I gained strength from them, the will to go another round. I made this mess, now I had to clean it up, and simply deal with it. I fell fast asleep.

(LOS ANGELES, CALIFORNIA; FRIDAY, NOVEMBER 13, 1992; 10:05 AM)

(OUTSIDE THE PRESENCE OF THE JURY)

The Clerk: United States of America vs. The Doctor. Counsel please state your appearance.

Mark: Mark for the government.

Reed: Good morning, your honor. Reed for The Doctor.

The Court: All right. I have a note from the jury: "Please send us Ben's testimony and FBI Agent Tim's testimony."

As you know gentlemen, we don't have a transcript to send in. So I intend to bring them into the courtroom and explain to them we don't have a transcript, that if there is any part of this testimony that's critical for their deliberations, we can have it read back by the reporter. But I'm told it will take about two hours to read back the testimony of Ben the informant.

Reed: Your honor, what if they say—of course, if there is a certain area with respect to Ben's testimony where the court reporter can scope into it, we would have no objection to having that testimony read back in open court in the presence of the Doctor.

The Court: Oh, sure.

Reed: But let's say they say, "we want it all read back."

The Court: Well, if they want it all read back, I'm going to have to give it to them.

Reed: Well, we oppose that. We would object to that, your honor.

The Court: Why?

Reed: Because we feel that they should rely on their collective memory of what occurred and that those particular areas shouldn't be re-emphasized, shouldn't be read back in its entirety.

The Court: well, okay.

Reed: We would object to that.

Mark: The government has—would agree with your honor's recommendation that if there are particular aspects of it they would like clarified, that that be read back. But I would agree with the defendant that if they want the entire testimony read back, that that's not appropriate.

The Court: Never heard any authority such as that. Is there any authority for that?

Mark: No, your honor, only that—

The Court: I have been a judge for many years. I have never heard that ever stated that it shouldn't be done.

Mark: Well, we're—

The Court: In other words—excuse me for interrupting you. But if a jury—you try to give a jury whatever they need to reach a fair and proper verdict.

Now, if they want something and you don't give it to them, then there is, I suppose, an argument that could be made, as Reed has just made, they have to rely on their own memories. Okay. That's an approach.

The other approach is, if they need it in order to reach a verdict, they should have it. So there are two lines of thought. I'm sure it's discretionary with the court. I don't think there is any rule that says I can't do it.

Mark: No. I'm certainly not aware of any. And I defer to the determination of the court.

The Court: Well, for instance, if they want it all read back, then I could tell them, no, they can't have it. Is that what you are suggesting?

Mark: Well, if it's in the court's determination that it's appropriate, however, to tell the jurors, "you ought to rely on your collective memories. If there are particular aspects that are in dispute and you would like the court reporter to attempt to find that aspect of the transcript and read it back to you, we can do that; but we are not going to replay the entire trial here and do it all over again for you."

The Court: All right So both of you, and I want the Doctor to agree on the record so there won't be any question on appeal that this was done without approval, I understand that the position of you, Reed, and you, Mark, is that if they want the entire testimony of Ben read back, the court should deny it. Is that correct?

Reed: Yes it is. And the Doctor—

The Court: Doctor, do you understand what we are talking about?

The Doctor: I would like to know what you mean in your last statement, you said, "so there won't be any question on appeal." I have not been found guilty. There is no appeal pending at this time, your honor. To answer your question, yes, I now do understand what is going on here.

97

The Court: Uh, I meant, I, uh, didn't mean appeal. I meant do you agree with your attorney that the court should not permit the entire testimony to be read back of our, I mean, the informant, Ben?

The Doctor: Yes, I agree with my attorney.

The Court: All right. So you have discussed this and this is a decision that you have made after being advised by your attorney and knowing that it could be totally read back?

The Doctor: Yes.

The Court: Call in the jury.

(WITHIN THE PRESENCE OF THE JURY)

The Court: Good morning ladies and gentlemen. I have a note from your foreperson, which reads: To judge please send to jurors Ben the informant's testimony, and the FBI agent's testimony.

Now, let's make something clear to you that perhaps wasn't made clear earlier. We have a court reporter here who takes down everything that is said during the trial; what anyone said, whether it is you, or the attorney's, or the judge. A witness, whoever it might be. But we do not have a transcript of that. She has notes that she can read from, but we do not have a transcript.

So it isn't as simple as just saying: We're going to send this in to you. We can't do that because we don't have such a transcript. And in fact, even if we did, there would be some question about whether you would be entitled to it.

Now, if there are certain parts of the testimony of Ben and Agent Tim that you want read back to you, the reporter can go through her notes and find that part or portion of the testimony that you feel you would like to hear again. So I don't know if that answers your question, but in order to read the testimony back, it would take probably two to three hours.

Juror Elmer: Don't you have an audio of this? Don't we have backup audio?

The Court: Oh, we have a tape, but that's not—the reporter uses a tape to support her if she is asked to do a transcript. If she has something in her notes that she, let's say, has some question about, she can go to her tape to see. But that tape is not part of the court's possession. It belongs to the court reporter and it is not an official record of any kind. So we don't use those in court, audios. There is no authorization of that.

There are I'm sure, some courts somewhere in the United States that may use the audio tapes that could be played back, but we don't use them here in this court.

Juror Lenny: We would like the prosecutor's examination of Ben, and the defense attorney's cross-examination of agent Tim.

The Court: Well, if you can specify what parts of the record you want read back, and then we can see about doing that; but to read it in its entirety is not acceptable. You have to rely on your own memories and notes. And the thing that always is troublesome is that if you concentrate just on one witness, then that may give greater emphasis to that testimony rather than the testimony of everyone else. And that's the danger in just repeating or reading back the testimony of one or two witnesses.

Juror Elmer: Are you making that as a point of law that you think that, since we all have mutually a desire to listen to these two witnesses, are you making that as a point of law that you don't feel that we should have—I don't want to use the word 'right' but there is some other terminology here, to listen to those even though we would give them, because of our questioning, more of a weight in this situation?

The Court: I said that is the danger in doing it. I'm not making any ruling as a matter of law in that respect. I'm just saying that argument will be made to this court, that by permitting the testimony of one or two witnesses to be read back in its entirety, that has lent too much emphasis to their testimony as opposed to the testimony of others. Now, I recognize what you are saying, and—

Juror Elmer: Can we get forebearance of both of the attorney's on this?

The Court: Well, I discussed this with the attorneys before you came into the courtroom, and I'm not at liberty to disclose to you what our discussions were. But yes, they are aware, of course, of your request. And I—in fact, I think— just so that I understand it, is it your feeling, Elmer, that the jury wants to hear all of the evidence or all of the testimony of those two witnesses?

Juror Elmer: That was our feeling.

The Court: Is that what all the jurors want?

(No response)

Juror Hepburn: I don't find it necessary that we listen to all that. Just the part of agent Tim in corroboration to what Ben had said to the FBI to corroborate credibility of Ben; do you agree? Because Ben said he is a liar, and his testimony was quite lengthy.

Juror Lenny: I would like the testimony of both.

The Court: I would like to have a side-bar conference with counsel.

(Side bar conference outside the hearing of the jury)

Reed: Your honor, I think the wisest thing to do is to let's rediscuss it amongst the three of us, out of the presence of the jury. It's kind of uncomfortable to be sitting here in front of them with them looking at our expressions as they are asking these questions and then make a decision as to what we'll do.

The Court: Okay.

(Within the hearing of the jury)

The Court: We are going to ask the jury to retire to the jury room again, and we are going to discuss this in greater length. And then it would be more convenient if we have you retire to the jury room, and then we will have you come back into the courtroom.

In the meantime, you might, as an alternative, write down the specifics of any of the testimony you would like read back, as an alternative, if you can do that. We'll summon you back in a few minutes.

(Outside the presence of the jury)

The Court: It seems to me that the great majority of them are pretty adamant about having the entire testimony read back, except one juror who spoke. Mark, what is your position?

Mark: It's clear to me, at least from the questioning, what the—I believe what the jurors are getting at, they want some kind of corroboration that Ben in fact met with the FBI and that he didn't just set the Doctor up on his own, or with Ben and Paul hiding the marijuana without the Doctor knowing. The marijuana was concealed, no smell, no visual. I'm not sure it's in the testimony, but they seem to think that the testimony of agent Tim, or the cross-examination of agent Tim is going to corroborate the fact that Ben in fact met with the FBI.

The Court: They seem to want the cross-examination rather than the direct.

Mark: I have no objection to just reading—to having just portions of agent Tim's testimony, even if it's only the cross-examination, read back. I have no objection to having portions of Ben's testimony read with respect to his meetings with the FBI.

I'm at somewhat of a loss here. I'm not—I will defer to the court. If the court thinks it's appropriate to read the entire testimony, I have no objection to that either. I think it can be achieved without doing that. But unless they are more specific in what they want, I'm not sure how we make that determination as to which portions of the transcript.

It's quite a burden on the court reporter to go through and find bits and pieces, whatever particular words were used, and I'm not sure how we do that either.

The Court: Well, she has done it many times before.

Reed: My position is that I do still object to the reading of the entire testimony of both witnesses. However, with respect to the cross-examination of agent Tim only, I would not object to the reading of that. However, who knows what they are going to send out in their next note.

The Court: Well, I think we'll give them a few minutes and see what, if anything, they can agree upon as to what they want read back. And if they come in with something they can agree upon, then that will make it easier to decide.

Mark: The problem we may have, your honor—and I don't want to anticipate what the jury is going to come back with—is that they may frame their questions in terms of points or issues that they want to hear testimony about.

And then there may be some argument as to whether or not particular testimony proves that point or disapproves that point. And it may be difficult for the court or for counsel, if the court wants our input, to parse out which portions of the testimony relate to the issues that they are concerned about. I suppose we'll just have to see what they come back with.

The Court: Well, that's always the problem when you pick and choose from a witness' testimony, portions of it. I don't know where this juror got the idea that we had an audio going. I guess he saw the court reporter's tape. Clerk, would you see if the jury needs more time? Reed, do you have any cases that say that its reversible error?

Reed: No.

The Clerk: They request a few more minutes.

Reed: I've seen this happen a few times in my career. And it's obviously discretionary to do whatever you want to do.

The Court: You know, when this has happened before, I have customarily had it read back because I've always been of the school that the juror's task is difficult enough without making it more difficult for them. If they want something read back to them, then it seems to me that in order to assist them in reaching a verdict that it should be read back. I know that there are people who disagree with that probably, but still I think that's—

Reed: Is that where the court is leaning if they say, well, we really want it all read back?

The Court: Yes.

Reed: Okay, we object for the record.

The Court: Yes, sure, whatever. But it will be helpful if they can narrow it down. Then what we'll have to do is have the reporter go through her notes and find out where the testimony is. And then one or the other of you may say, well, there is other testimony relating to this point that's somewhere in the record, and we'll have to go and search it even further. So it might take longer to search the record than it would be to read it. I don't have any idea. But it being such a short trial, I'm a little surprised, frankly, that this has come up. We just heard this testimony on Tuesday. Was it Tuesday or Wednesday?

Reed: Tuesday.

Mark: Late in the day.

The Court: Yeah, right. Well, I'm going to my chambers.

(RECESS)

During the recess, all I could do was watch all the players do whatever they do. I asked Reed some elementary questions. Reed prepared notes, and asked me a couple questions, which he already knew the answer to. I was tired, stressed, and hungry. Sitting, just sitting and listening all day. I had no idea of the outcome; I just knew that Reed had the jury questioning each other. I had a chance.

(LOS ANGELES, CALFORNIA; FRIDAY, NOVEMBER 13TH, 1992; 11:55 AM-WITHIN THE PRESENCE OF THE JURY)

The Court: Ladies and gentlemen, I have a note from your foreperson. It reads: "The jury requests the following: Defense attorney's questioning of Ben the informant in response to association and contacts with the Doctor." That's the testimony you would like to hear?

Juror carol: That's correct.

The Court: So that would be the cross-examination of Ben the informant?

Juror Carol: That's correct.

The Court: It would be found there?

Juror Carol: We believe so.

The Court: All right. So the reporter will have to search her notes. In the meantime, you will be taken to lunch. And when you get back, maybe then she will have been able to extract that testimony and we'll have it read back to you.

Juror Carol: How long of a lunch period are you contemplating?

The Court: As long as it takes you to eat.

Juror Carol: Do we go eat on our own?

The Court: No, once you deliberate, you stay together.

(OUTSIDE THE PRESENCE OF THE JURY)

The Court: Reporter, how long is it going to take you to read?

Mark: Is it the court's intention to have the court reporter only read back portions of the cross-examination that relate to the defendant's contact with Ben the informant, or also portions of the direct examination from me.

The Court: They didn't ask for the direct from you.

Mark: They must want my direct. I'm the prosecutor. Why wouldn't they want the direct?

The Court: I have no idea. Maybe they remember it. You can stay here and assist the reporter if you want. We are now in noon recess.

(NOON RECESS)

I was lead back downstairs to the holding area. A bologna sandwich, chips, and an apple were my lunch. The apple was ok. I had no idea what was going on with this case. The jury was arguing amongst themselves. Reed was proud of himself for this. Mark was whining. The reporter did her job. The Marshal's didn't care either way. I waited patiently. I read the graffiti scratched into the layers of paint on the walls. Sleep was out of the question; comfort was out of the question. I was alone in the large cell. No other prisoners were in the immediate area. I just waited.

(LOS ANGELES, CALIFORNIA; FRIDAY, NOVEMBER 13TH, 1992; 1:30PM—OUTSIDE THE PRESENCE OF THE JURY—DEFENDANT IS PRESENT)

The Court: All right. You wanted to take up a couple matters before we bring in the jury in.

Reed: Right, your honor. There are portions of the cross-examination that Mark wants read back to the jury that I don't want read back. The first area that I do not want read back but that Mark does has to do with my opening examination concerning: "What type of notes did you review in coming to court? Did these notes have to do with your interactions concerning the Doctor?" He wants those read. I don't think that those are directly pertinent and probative on the actual meetings. I don't want to speak for Mark.

Mark: Let me just—I don't mean to interrupt. But just on this one issue, just to make sure we are clear. I don't want all the questions read about the notes. There were one-maybe two questions on—basically referring to the time period of the meetings with the Doctor. And those are the only questions I would want.

Reed: Well, I don't—I think that all those time-frame questions have to do with—

The Court: I don't know what they want. They have something in mind, I suppose, in making their request. So I'm going to have the reporter read what she selected with Mark, and you can go on the record, either now or later. Specifically I'm going to ask the jury, after they have heard her reading, whether or not this covers the subject or the area that they are interested in. And if not, we'll go further. If it does, we will let it go at that.

Reed: So I take it then the court is just going to allow all those areas, which are disputed between the two parties to be read?

The Court: Yes. Summon the jury. Reporter, you will read from the witness stand.

The reporter read the portions of the cross-examination that her and the prosecutor agreed on during lunch. The jury listened, nodded, and listened some more. They were finally satisfied and retired for final deliberations. I was escorted back down to the holding cell. I waited, and waited for the jury to reach a verdict.

(LOS ANGELES, CALIFORNIA; FRIDAY, NOVEMBER 13TH, 1992; 2:40 PM—WITHIN THE PRESENCE OF THE JURY)

The Court: All right. Ladies and gentlemen, I have a note from your foreperson that you have reached a verdict. Is that correct?

Juror Carol: Correct

The Court: Would you give the verdict form to the Bailiff?

Juror Carol: We already handed it to him.

The Bailiff: Uh, what, the verdict form?

Juror Carol: Yes.

The Court: No, I have the note from the jury; I don't have the verdict form.

Juror Carol: I think you do judge.

(DOCUMENT HANDED TO THE COURT)

The Court: See, see, I have this document, which says, "note from the jury." The verdict is the paper with the name of the case on it and all that stuff.

Juror Carol: Then we need that paperwork.

The Court: well, here is a copy of the verdict form. Hand this to the foreperson.

Juror Carol: We have one in the jury room.

The Court: You think you have that?

Juror Carol: I think there may be one of those in there.

The Court: Then why don't you all retire and complete that form, and I'll wait here for you.

(THE JURORS LEAVE THE COURTROOM)

The Court: This is off the record now.

(OFF THE RECORD DISCUSSION)

The Court: All right. Juror, do you have the correct form now?

Juror Carol: I sure do.

The Court: Hand it to the clerk.

The Clerk: "United States District Court, Central District of California. Criminal Case Number, United States of America vs. The Doctor. Verdict. "We, the jury in the above titled cause, find the defendant 'The Doctor' guilty as charged in the indictment." Signed by the foreperson, Carol. Ladies and gentlemen of the jury, is this as presented and read the verdict of each of you, so say you one, say you all?

The Jurors: Yes.

The Court: Why don't you poll the jury?

The Clerk: If this is your verdict answer yes.

Juror: Yes.

Juror: Yes.

Juror: Yes.

Juror: Yes.

Juror: Yes, I'm sorry.

Juror: Yes.

Juror: Yes.

Juror: Yes.

Juror: Yes.

Juror: Yes.

Juror: Yes.

Juror: Yes.

The middle aged, black nurse from South Central Los Angeles told me she was sorry. She was sincere.

The Court: Enter the verdict.

Ladies and gentlemen, you are no longer under any admonition of this court about talking to anyone about this case. If you wish to talk to someone about it, you may do so. The court releases you. Thank you.

Juror Elmer: Can we talk to an agent about our movie rights?

Juror Lenny: Yeah, what about a movie contract? Do we get royalties?

The Court: Uh, you may talk to anyone you want. Dismissed.

Juror Elmer: We do get royalties, for this if this becomes a movie. Elmer said as the Bailiff escorted him from the room.

(OUTSIDE THE PRESENCE OF THE JURY)

The Court: We will order a presentence report, Reed, and you will set the matter down for judgment and sentencing on—

The Clerk: January 25th at 3:00 PM

Mark: Your Honor, Paul his co-defendant is scheduled to be sentenced on the 18th. I'm not sure if it makes sense to schedule them at the same time. There's no problem, as far as I'm concerned, to do them on separate days; but, at the court's convenience, we would like to keep the matters together.

Reed: we would like the 18th too, your honor.

The Court: Ok, the 18th, it is. The Doctor will remain in custody.

Mark: Is it necessary for the court to advise the Doctor of his appeal rights?

Reed: No, it is not necessary, on sentencing day.

Mark: Oh, uh, ok.

The Court: I haven't imposed judgment yet.

Mark: Uh, oh, sorry, I apologize. I just wanted to make sure.

(PROCEEDINGS ADJOURNED)

Now, the big hurry up and wait began. I was moved from my room on the ninth floor, to a floor filled with 130 men waiting to be sentenced, and shipped to prisons around the country. My new cellmate Bill was waiting for transfer to a prison. He was doing a three-year term for conspiracy to murder someone, or a lot of people. I never knew.

Phone calls to home were hard. I knew I was facing ten years. I had been waiting in MDC for nine months. I wouldn't get to a prison until, at least March sometime. I was healthy, my mind was sharp. I played cards, chess, I worked out, I wrote letters, and I kept notes of my daily activities. I ate the best I could. I encountered no problems with other inmates. I had seen my fill of violence in the room, and this was just the beginning.

Staying close to family and friends was difficult. I had no visits. Letters from my girlfriend Meg were on time. I knew, this wouldn't last. Anyone who thinks a marriage or relationship will stay the same after anytime in prison is very ignorant. We are the ones inside, they are free to do as they please, get used to it quickly. Stress will kill you inside of prison.

I ran across the best cribbage, and chess players in the world inside the walls of MDC. We had nothing else to do except perfect the little things in life.

Thanksgiving, Christmas, New Years, went by in a blur. Receiving X-mas cards in the mail was the best. My sentencing date had been changed to February 8th, 1993. I didn't mind the wait; I had to do my time somewhere, here, there, it didn't matter. I had no idea when Paul's sentencing would be. I just knew I had more opportunity and activity inside a prison. A prison is a small community, within a community.

(LOS ANGELES, CALIFORNIA; MONDAY, FEBRUARY 8TH, 1993)

The Clerk: United States of America vs. The Doctor.

The Court: Counsel, please state your appearance.

Mark: Mark again for the government.

Reed: Good afternoon, your honor. Reed on behalf of the Doctor. He's present in court.

The Court: All right. The matter is here for the purpose of judgment and sentencing. I've read the pre-sentence report. I've read Reed's objection to the enhancement application. And I presume you have read it also, Mark?

Mark: Yes, your honor. I received a copy of it late this morning. First of all, I'd like to point out just one factual inconsistency that I noted in reed's declaration. There is a copy of a signed plea agreement attached as an Exhibit bearing a date of May 12th, 1992 and apparently signed by the Doctor but not by his attorney at the time attorney Trevino.

The Court: May 12th or 7th?

Mark: The letter is dated May 7th. It bears a signature date of May 12th.

The Court: Oh, all right.

Mark: And I'm not sure when the Doctor signed that. I have no reason to believe he did not sign it on the 12th. Just wanted to point out for the court that I was never provided with a signed copy by Trevino.

Trevino set out in a declaration on May 19th that was submitted to the court in connection with his request to be relieved as counsel, he set out in that declaration the fact that it was the Doctor's intent to plead guilty and that he had learned the previous day by virtue of Paul's attorney's motion that Paul was not going to plead guilty and therefore that the deal offered by the government was not going to be accepted. So that was the contact that the government had with Trevino on the issue of that plea. It learned for the first time in that same week the Doctor wanted to plead guilty, Paul did not. But there was never an exchange of plea agreement. So on the factual issue I'm not really sure it's significant here but I just wanted to point out that issue.

I was made aware at some point that the Doctor wanted to accept the plea but was never given a signed plea agreement. The plea letter it's clear that it was based on both defendants' accepting it. The reason for that—your honor, I'll just go into them very briefly—had to do with the ex parte application that the government filed to keep certain matters confidential until another investigation was finished that had to do with the confidential informant Ben's role in the case. The defendant's did not know that Ben was the informant at this time of the agreement.

The government in light of the fact that information was highly sensitive, the government made what it considered to be a very generous plea offer early on in the case. Both defendants's had to accept it so that the government wouldn't have to go forward with the motion to suppress and reveal that information. And that was the reason why it was a package deal, if you will. When both defendant's did not agree, the government revoked the offer and went forward with the motion to suppress. One of the defendant's pled and the Doctor went to trial.

The Court: Did your plea agreement provide that both of them had to plead?

Mark: Yes, your honor. In the first paragraph of the plea agreement it refers to defendant's collectively. In the last—excuse me. The second to the last sentence of that paragraph says: "This offer is contingent upon both of you accepting the offer. If you do not both accept the offer by May 15th it is automatically withdrawn," and that's what happened.

Secondly, I would note, your honor, that the Doctor was not prejudiced in this case by the government withdrawing the plea. It wasn't as if he pled guilty and the government changed the terms of the deal on him in this case. He was essentially left in the same position he would have been had the government never extended any offer by going to trial.

Reed: Your honor, for clarification of the record on this specific issue. Whether or not the plea agreement—

The Court: Excuse me—are you two back there in the courtroom—why don't you two sit down if you're going to stay and listen to this—would you do that please? (The judge said this to my co-defendant Paul who walked into the courtroom with a curvy; I guess you could say, red headed lady who appeared to be our age. My attorney Reed told me that Paul's sentencing date was postponed until February 14th, Valentines Day, because Paul was going to Reno, Nevada to marry this "curvy" redhead. Now, back to my proceedings.)

Reed: On this issue of whether or not the plea agreement was physically handed over to the government or physically handed to the court in open court, I cannot state to the court in a declaration whether it was or not because I wasn't the attorney representing the Doctor at the time.

The Court: What difference would that make?

Reed: Well, your honor, perhaps on appeal if the court looks at the equities of the situation, if they feel that perhaps a plea agreement was actually turned over to the court, filed with the court wherein the Doctor accepted it, that it would maybe have more moral weight. He might be in a stronger position to argue that he at all times definitely accepted this offer. It's not his fault that the co-defendant wanted to run the motion to suppress. And so I felt that that was a factor that would be important to the reviewing court.

This issue of whether or not it was physically turned over to the clerk of your court or to the government. The Doctor has indicated to me that that plea agreement was signed by him and it was actually turned over to the court in open court.

The Court: Why wasn't it signed by his attorney?

Reed: I have no idea.

The Court; I mean, usually it's at least my practice to look at any agreement that's handed up to me to see that it's signed not only by the defendant but by his attorney, otherwise it's really not a complete document in my eyes. And I can't recall—and, of course, I'm just going from memory now. I cannot recall ever seeing a plea letter in this case signed by the Doctor, period.

Reed: I thought that maybe the court might have its own files that it keeps of cases, files that are different.

The Court: The clerk I think probably files it. Clerk, what do you do with those plea letters, do you put them in the master file?

The clerk: I file them but I keep them in your file so if there is one you'd have it.

The Court: Well, my clerk advises me that she—if she takes the plea letter she puts it in our court file, not the file in the clerk's office. And I haven't searched through the file to see if one's here.

Mark: Your honor, to some extent I'm going from my memory as well and also from my notes on the file jacket which indicates that the only time we were in court between defendant's pleas of not guilty and the Doctor's first attorney Trevino's withdrawl of counsel on May 20th, 1992 was on April 24th when Paul had a bail review hearing. There was not a—I was not in court on this matter and I certainly don't recall handing any plea agreement to the court. If the defendant filed that on his own I have no way of knowing.

The Court: I don't see any such letter in the file, Reed. I'm just looking at the declaration Trevino filed when he was relieved of counsel because of an upcoming death penalty appeal he was working on, to see if there was any reference made in that.

Mark: Your honor, there is a reference in paragraph 4 of that declaration which states that—excuse me, paragraphs 4, 5 and 6 which states that the Doctor fully intended to accept the government's plea offer and that Paul did not. And the government is certainly willing to concede to that point.

Whether or not the Doctor actually signed an agreement, it seems clear that he intended to and did desire to accept the plea offer. However, as I've noted, it was a— the offer was contingent upon both defendant's accepting.

The Court: Well, he does say that he discussed the case with the Doctor and it was clear to Trevino that he— The Doctor—decided to accept the plea offer that the government had extended and he didn't believe the case would consume any amount of his time.

(Reading)Then he said that the plea offer was contingent upon both defendants accepting the offer. However, it was not until yesterday, Monday, May 18th, 1992, that I had learned that the co-defendant had decided definitely not to accept the offer. Instead, yesterday through his counsel he filed a motion to suppress evidence and intends to litigate the issue.

(Reading) Says the principle and almost sole incentive the government can off the Doctor in this case is to forego filing an enhancement regarding his prior narcotic conviction. The government had agreed to do so pursuant to the earlier plea offer, yet it was noted that the offer was contingent upon the co-defendant agreeing to plead guilty. The offer has now been revoked. For this reason the Doctor now has every incentive to join his co-defendant in litigating any pre-trial motions as well as pursuing this matter to trial.

(Reading) Discussed these matters with the Doctor as well as the relative advantages and disadvantages of his accepting the plea offer. At the conclusion of those discussions with the Doctor determined he would accept the offer and forego litigating the matters before this court. However, since the government would not permit him alone to accept the plea offer he no longer has any incentive to forego the litigation.

That's the only evidence I see in the file of any letter. There is no plea letter.

Reed: Even so, your honor, it comes down to a concern for I guess two specific issues. The first concern is of the appropriateness of offering collective plea agreements to defendants by the government wherein unless they both plead guilty they're going to have to go to trial. We feel that that's an unfair practice.

But the second specific issue would be is offering a collective plea agreement under circumstances where crucial facts are hidden from the defendants so that they can make an intelligent decision on whether or not to enter a plea. I have a great deal of concern with respect to the offering of collective plea agreements, in the first place. But that concern is definitely compounded when the government does it in such a way wherein crucial facts are withheld.

And I don't think there is any dispute in this case concerning the fact that crucial facts were withheld, which led Paul's attorney to feel that there was a viable suppression motion. And if those facts had been told—and they didn't have to be told in such a way where the government says to Paul's attorney and myself, "we have an informant that's involved in this case." All they would have to do—

The Court: What were the crucial facts?

Reed: The crucial facts were that there was an informant involved in the investigation of the Doctor and Paul well before they went on their Mexico trip. And he interacted with these individuals over a considerable period of time. He had been, in my understanding, a tested informant. And he had not only interacted in such a detailed way which would have definitely provided probable cause for any search by the Coast Guards at a later time, but interacted to the extent where he implanted an electronic tracking device within the sailboat so that the Coast Guard could monitor.

Now, at the time that Paul's attorney made his decision to run a motion to suppress, he made that decision just based on the bare search that was made by the Coast Guard out at sea beyond the jurisdiction of the United States, without an administrative order issued for that search, and did not know anything about this informant.

Now, I've spoken with Paul's attorney many times and we've always agreed that had he known about this informant he would have never ran that suppression motion. The Doctor would have pled guilty, so would Paul. In fact, Paul did plead guilty after we ran the suppression motion which corroborates the fact that he would have pled guilty had he known about the informant earlier and we wouldn't be in this unfair situation wherein as a result of withholding that information now the Doctor has to suffer.

The Court: Couldn't the Doctor have pled guilty before the trial after the motion to suppress? When Paul entered his plea the government wouldn't accept the Doctor's plea at that time. Is that what you are saying?

Reed: Well, what happened as soon as Paul's attorney decided to run that motion to suppress shortly thereafter and before the motion was heard I believe the government came in with the information. They filed the information and indicated that if this motion was going to be run the ball game is over; we're going to file that information

117

and if you lose that suppression motion—and all the while keeping all these pertinent facts from us. If you lose this motion your guy the Doctor is going to have to plead now to a situation where there is an enhancement and he's got to get a MANDATORY/MINIMUM 10 years. And so we would have been forced into pleading guilty wherein he had to go to prison for a MANDATORY/MINIMUM 10 years.

The Court: Paul isn't gaining anything by way of the plea agreement either, is he?

Reed: Yes. The earlier plea agreement withheld the filing of the enhancement. He would have been able to plead and get a MANDATORY/MINIMUM 5-year sentence. Because the guideline range would have been a 26 as is outlined in the probation report with a level 2. That would have—and it would have come down to a level 24 for two points acceptance of responsibility and would have brought him very close to a MANDATORY/MINIMUM five years sentence. And he wanted to take it and he would have taken it. But as soon, as I say, as Paul's attorney filed that suppression motion the offer was withdrawn or was withdrawn shortly after the time period as outlined in the plea agreement I believe may 15th or something. And they never did go back to that original offer.

In fact, your honor, I think, Mark, who was a very honorable assistant—I've handled many cases with Mark— was a little troubled and concerned about the entire situation, too. Because after we ran the motion and I had at that point found out about the informant, which was withheld by the government 'cause they didn't want to blow his cover, so to speak, Mark, was good enough, feeling a little bit guilty perhaps at that point, and good enough going up to his supervisors asking whether or not the offer could be remade to the Doctor in the interest of fair of fair play. Mark did go up and check with his supervisors and I believe the answer was given that the Doctor could no longer be given the benefit of the earlier plea agreement. He ran the motion to suppress and it's to late.

The Court: Why did you let Paul plead before enhancement and then enhance and then refuse to let this--?

Mark: Your honor, the difference was Paul did not have a prior felony conviction. So early on Paul was looking at a MANDATORY/MINIMUM 5 year sentence based on the amount of drugs involved. The Doctor, with his prior conviction was looking at a 10 year MANDATORY/MINIMUM.

The government decided on the outset that there was very little we could off Paul because he was looking at a 5 year MANDATORY/MINIMUM regardless of what you might decide. MANDATORY/MINIMUM sentencing overrides any court decision.

With respect to the Doctor the government had the ability and made the decision to withhold the enhancement in order to dispose of the case quickly and not jeopardize the identity and the safety of the confidential informant Ben C------r.

The Court: Without the enhancement what would it have been, five?

Mark: Yes. And he would have been in the same boat as—pardon the pun—as Paul.

Now, Paul declined the offer because, he thought he would beat this case. It doesn't surprise me that the Doctor took this substantial offer, substantial reduction of sentence.

The only thing to the extent the—and I'm sure Reed didn't intend to do this. To the extent government conduct here is being portrayed as somehow vindictive that the Doctor—the deal was pulled after the Doctor decided to pursue the motion to suppress. It's clearly not the case. As the court is aware, the reason for the offer was dispose of the case quickly and not have to jeopardize the confidential informant. Once the motion to suppress was opposed—part of the opposition was disclosing the existence of the tracking device and the existence of the confidential informant. Once that had been disclosed there was no real reason for the government to persist in its offer and that's why it was revoked at that time.

Reed: And if we had known about the confidential informant both parties would have disposed of it. But they withheld that information.

Mark: Your honor, had the confidential informant's identity been known the government would never have made the offer. There would be no reason to.

Reed: They wouldn't have even had to do that. I've worked so often with the United States Attorney's office. If one of their assistants would have told me: Reed, we have information which we can't reveal to you which we assure you will result in your losing a suppression motion, but we can't reveal it, it has to do with previous investigations taking place, they wouldn't have had to tell me about an informant or identity. I think Paul's attorney and myself would have disposed of the case at the earliest possible moment. But they didn't tell us anything about the existence of any other information, which would have been disastrous to running a suppression motion.

The Court: If they didn't both agree and all bets were off and the offer was withdrawn, where did that leave Paul when he made his plea?

Mark: Paul pled straight up to the indictment. The government will recommend acceptance of responsibility be plead on the day of trial. And so presumably—probation recommended that we have an offense level of 26 minus 2 points for acceptance and the government concurs.

The Court: So he gained nothing from the plea agreement?

Mark: There was no plea agreement. Paul pled in the absence of a plea agreement.

Your honor, just briefly. As far as legal guidance on this issue the closest I could come—and it's quite close. It's not in our circuit, however—is a third circuit case called U.S. versus Gonzales, where the government offered a package deal. One of the defendants refused to accept the agreement and the other defendant claimed that it was a violation of their due process rights by conditioning the plea agreement on acceptance by all three defendants. The third circuit in that case said it was not a violation of either any contractual obligation on the part of the government or due process obligations.

The court said (Reading) "That agreement was never reached, the proposal was withdrawn and the agreement was never presented to the district court. It's axiomatic that a plea agreement is either binding nor enforceable till it is accepted in open court." That's precisely what we have in this case, your honor.

Reed: Except perhaps in that case they told the defendants what the nature of the evidence was against them.

The Court: Well, you know, I hear what you are saying. But I guess the thing I question is why is it the government has a duty to tell you what their evidence is going to be on a motion to suppress.

Is there duty on their part to disclose that?

Reed: I think under the circumstances where they offer a collective plea agreement and they determine that one of the defendant's wants to run the motion but the other one doesn't, and they are withholding the information to the detriment—the ultimate detriment of the person who wants to accept it, it could perhaps be considered a violation of that person's due process rights under all the circumstances. By withholding the information, which would lead the other defendant to not accept it, to the detriment of the poor defendant who wants to get the case over and accept his responsibility.

I know about collective plea agreements and I know that they have been upheld. But this is a different situation, a situation where had we been told—not asking that it had to rise to the level of being given details, just told that there was no possible way that the motion to suppress could be run— Paul would not have run the motion. We would have all accepted that earlier collective plea agreement.

The Court: I know that's what you say now. But this is after trial and after the defendant's been found guilty by a jury. I hear what you are saying. But I suppose what else would you say other than that at this point. I mean, it's obvious that that's the position you have to take and I don't fault you for it. I mean, I can see there were some problems here with the plea.

But if the plea had been taken under this plea agreement with Paul then I would totally agree with you, but apparently it wasn't. The plea was totally outside the proposed plea agreement in the letter.

Reed: Although Paul—although he may not have signed the plea agreement, it's my understanding that the government is recommending exactly everything that he would have gotten by executing the plea agreement. It's my understanding that by Paul pleading guilty the government's recommending 2-point level for acceptance of responsibility. So therefore, the effect of what he's been allowed to plead to is identical to what the plea agreement is.

The Court: That may be true. Is there any—

Mark: That is true, your honor.

Reed: So he lost nothing by running that motion to suppress.

The Court: I guess the agreement was directed toward the Doctor instead of Paul.

What you're asking me to do, Reed, if I understand it, is to somehow or another find the government was at fault for not letting the Doctor plead and therefore sentence him under the indictment before it was enhanced. Is that what you're saying?

Reed: Yes, your honor, exactly.

The Court: And that results in the same sentence then for the Doctor as Paul with the exception that he has a prior?

Reed: Right, your honor. He's going to—he would get more time. Because Paul doesn't have a prior. I don't believe Paul's in a category 2. But the Doctor—if the court were to do that, the level would be as calculated within the probation report, a level 26, with a category 2 which would result in a 70m to 87 month range; significantly less than a MANDATORY/MINIMUM 10 years.

Mark: Your honor, I see the kind of facial appeal of such a sentence or such a ruling in that the defendants would be sentenced relatively closely.

However, what the defendant is really asking for here is that the court order the government to extend an offer that the government has chosen not to extend.

It's clear that the government can—could have decided not to make any plea offer in this case. It's clear that the government could make a plea offer and set a deadline that it considers appropriate and adhere to that deadline.

And what the defendant is saying here is that the government should—notwithstanding its reason, whether legitimate or illegitimate, for its decision to make an offer the government should be stuck with that offer that was never contractually accepted and the courts have viewed these agreements in contractual terms.

The Court: Well, the thing that's troublesome is that Reed says had you told them that you have a confidential

123

informant—you didn't have to identify him, just told him that you had one—then he would have pled guilty.

Mark: Two points there, your honor.

First of all, the government's concern was that the mere revelation of the existence of an informant would have made clear who the informant was. And that's what we pointed out in the ex parte papers that we filed requesting that the motion to suppress be continued for a month so that we can finish the other investigation.

Secondly, if we had disclosed that fact the government wouldn't have even made the offer. The only reason to make the offer which our office considered—before declining to file an enhancement our office and my understanding is department of justice has very strict guidelines as to when we can withhold these enhancements so that it's not done on a case-by-case basis with inconsistent results. But there has to be some compelling reason why the Doctor would be treated differently than someone else with a prior felony drug conviction.

A determination was made that the ongoing investigation was sensitive enough and was important enough that the government would treat the Doctor differently than it does most defendants with prior drug convictions. And that was the determination that was made. Once that factor disappeared our office felt compelled—and Reed is right. I did go to my supervisors and ask if we could withhold the enhancement. But the determination was this case should be treated like every other case.

The Court: Was there any reason why you didn't ask for enhancement when the original indictment was filed?

Mark: My understanding of office policy is that at some point after indictment but prior to trial as soon as it's confirmed that the defendant has a prior conviction, then the enhancement or the information is filed. And the only reason that I withheld doing that was because I knew it offered a possibility of perhaps a quick plea to conceal the identity of the informant. And then I knew once we filed the enhancement there would be no chance of a plea in the case.

The Court: Well, reed, I don't really see that the court has any reason—even though I can understand your concern. I don't see that the court has any grounds on which to do what you're asking, even though I fully appreciate what you're telling me. But that's the way the government proceeded and I don't know that there is any rule or regulation or law or case, or any authority that says they can't do it this was. I mean, maybe it's not the best way to do it, but that's what they have done here. And they are within the boundaries of law and procedures.

I don't think that the court can just say that it wasn't because of the government's actions that they have violated the law, custom and practice. I don't know if this has ever come about. I've never had this situation presented to me before.

So I'm not going to grant the motion to eliminate the enhancement.

Reed: We are ready to proceed, your honor. Thank you for hearing us at length. We appreciate that very much. This has a great deal of trouble and concern to me.

The Court: I can see.

Reed: I feel that it's just not right. It's unfair. But I appreciate the court hearing this.

The Court: You've done your best to lay out your position and I'm sure that it was the very best you could do.

Well, first of all, is there any factual recitation in the pre-sentence report that you would like to address as being incorrect?

Reed: No, your honor.

The Court: Doctor, is there any factual recitation in there that you would like to object to?

The Doctor: No.

The Court: The court will then adopt the factual recitation. Do you wish to be heard on the matter as far as sentencing is concerned, that is, beyond what we've said already, Reed?

Reed: The Doctor does not want to say anything. And the only thing that I would ask, your honor, is that the judgment and commitment order reflect the court's recommendation that the Doctor do his prison time in the Minnesota area. That's where his family is from.

The Court: All right. Doctor, you have no statement you would like to make?

The Doctor: No.

The Court: Mark, do you have anything to say.

Mark: No.

The Court: Is there any legal cause why sentence should not now be imposed?

Reed: No, your honor.

The Court: The Doctor waives formal arraignment for judgment and sentence?

Reed: Yes.

The Court: Well, based upon the sentence reform act of 1984 and the statute, 21 USC 960(B), subsection 2, there is a —and also having in mind the guideline provisions of total offense level of 26 with a criminal history category of 2, we have under 5(G) 1.1(B) a MANDATORY/MINIMUM sentence of 120 months. That will be the judgment and sentence of the court.

The defendant, the Doctor, is committed on the single-count indictment to the custody of the bureau of prisons to be imprisoned for a term of 120 months.

Upon release from imprisonment the defendant shall be placed on supervised release for a term of eight years on the following terms and conditions:

That the defendant shall comply with the rules and regulations of the United States probation office and general order 318. Pursuant to section 5(E) 1.2(F) of the guidelines all fines are waived, including the cost of imprisonment and supervision.

It is further ordered the defendant shall pay to the United States a special assessment of $50.00.

The justification for this sentence is that this is the defendant's second conviction for narcotics related offense. In the instant case the defendant was found aboard a vessel, which contained over 200 kilograms of marijuana, which had been picked up in Mexico and was being transported back to the Los Angeles area.

Previously the defendant had been arrested in Florida in 1984 for transporting marijuana aboard a vessel departing from the country of Colombia. And that time he was involved with over a thousand pounds of marijuana. He received a 5-year custody sentence with the attorney general for that conviction.

The government has filed a motion alleging the defendant's prior conviction for a narcotics-related offense to enhance the defendant's sentence in the instant matter. Therefore, although the defendant's guideline range would have been 70 to 87 months, the defendant's MANDATORY/MINIMUM sentence is 120 months with 8 years of supervised release. Therefore, the MANDATORY/MINIMUM sentence of imprisonment shall become the guideline sentence.

It appears that the previous conviction and sentence did not sufficiently punish or deter the defendant from committing this crime or future crimes and it is hoped that this sentence will serve as a sufficient punishment and deterrent.

Doctor, the court must advise you of your rights on appeal. You have the right to appeal the judgment and sentence of the court. If you wish to appeal you must file your notice of appeal within 10 days of today's date. You file your notice of appeal in the clerk's office on the main street level of this building.

There is a filing fee that's required. If you don't have the funds to pay the court will order them waived.

If you don't have the funds to hire an attorney on appeal the court will consider appointing you one.

And Reed, if there is going to be an appeal the court orders you to see to it that it's timely filed.

Reed: I will. Could the judgment and commitment order reflect a recommendation to Minnesota?

The Court: Oh, yes. The court will recommend that the Doctor be committed to an institution in the state of— Minnesota, was it?

Reed: Yes.

The Court: Minnesota. Or as close thereto as possible.

Reed: Thank you.

The Court: Okay. Very well. That will be the judgment of the court.

EPILOGUE

After the sentencing, Hank, the U.S. Marshal who was assigned to my case since the trial, put handcuffs on me, like he had done so many times before. Hank was retiring soon. He even looked like old man Fonda. The courtroom players were filing papers, walking here and there gathering who knows what. Briefcases snapped shut. Reed, looked at me sincerely. He did his best. We parted as friends. Mark, the prosecutor looked me in the eye and nodded a good bye. Paul and his curvy girlfriend walked out hand in hand. Paul told me he was sorry for not accepting the plea agreement. I told him it was part of the game.

Hank and I turned and walked out the side door of the courtroom. "Doctor, you did your trial and sentencing with honor, and dignity. You didn't snitch, you didn't whine and snivel. You will be ok," Hank said as we walked toward the holding cell. "Hank, how about we walk up to the main street level. The judge said I could file my appeal with the clerks office," I said as Hank uncuffed me inside the empty cell. "Doctor, I would let you walk right now, if I could," Hank said as he summoned the jailer. The jailer handed him a paper bag that said Fatburger on it. Fatburger is a local L.A. fantastic burger place. "Here you go, Doctor. I know you aren't going to tell on me," he said winking as he walked away. I ate the food and savored every bite. I wouldn't eat street food for the next eight and a half years.

Mandatory/Minimum sentences are set for you to do eighty five percent of the time. Are these fair sentences for drug crimes? A lot of people will argue, and snivel about this. I personally will not snivel. I would like to see the death penalty for child molesters of any degree.

The drug business in any capacity is a crapshoot. This is simple. If you play the drug game, do your research. As you have found out by reading my three book series. It is your friends, co-defendant's, people closest to you, and in some peoples cases even family members, who bring you to justice. Remember, agents in all capacities do not know about you, until someone tells on you. Agents even become annoyed with snitches. You can trust no one, no one, in the drug business, ever. I have seen first hand, the toughest guys, and ladies in the drug business, are the first ones to turn tail and run, then snitch. You have no friends in the drug business, period.

I started my ten-year sentence in Terra Haute, Indiana Penitentiary. This penitentiary houses all types of criminals. With a ten-year sentence, I was called 'shorttime.' A ten-year sentence compared to life, even twenty-year sentences is light. Remember, three strikes and your out. Well, they are in there, and my third strike would be next. I have no intention of this life.

I was soon transferred to Oxford, Wisconsin, FCI. Federal Correctional Institution. This is a Medium/High level facility located in central Wisconsin. As time goes on, your custody/security level goes down, if you don't have any incident reports, i.e. drug use, violence, etc. This will enhance your sentence.

A year later I was transferred to Rochester, FMC. Federal Medical Center, located in southern, Minnesota. Rochester is a very well run Federal Prison Medical facility. Prisoners are sent here for evaluations, medical and mental. Serious medical operations are performed here, and the hospice ward is full. I was transferred here to fill a position on the 200-man work cadre. We would tend to orderly work, such as my pal Tim from South Bend, Indiana did. He would walk medical prisoners around the yard for exercise, or to just let them get a view of the sky. He worked in the psych ward. I did landscaping; others did food service, janitor work, and basic prison up keep. Being this close to Minneapolis made visiting easier for family and friends. My entire family and friends outside the drug business stood by me.

A few years later I was considered a low level prisoner. I was transferred to a Prison Camp, in Duluth, Minnesota, located along the Lake Superior shoreline. This was an abandoned Air Force base. We had no fences around us. A movie theater, bowling alley, and soft mattresses made life a bit more comfortable. This was hard time, because these camps are filled with first time offenders, who think they are in a penitentiary, and snitches that are being hidden. I worked in food service. Three tough kids doing a hard, one-year sentence for possession of crack cocaine, thought they would disrespect me in the food service office one evening. There was a guard in the office where I worked. The one kid about 21 years of age mouthed off something I couldn't really understand. I asked the guard to excuse me, he lifted his legs from the desk, and I punched the kid in the nose. He went down, the other two fled yelling back that they would get me. The guard hit his emergency button, and I was immediately handcuffed. That is how it is done in prison when you are out numbered. Just use the surprise tactic. It works every time. The kids thought I wouldn't do anything because a guard was there. They were wrong.

Now, after 44 days in the 'hole' aka segregation. A cell alone away from everyone. I was on a disciplinary transfer to Sandstone, FCI. Sandstone is a dumping ground for disciplinary prisoners. I knew a handful of prisoners when I got there. It was like old home week. It was good to get out of that silly little camp.

I worked in the commissary. A great job, if you can get it. Short work hours, with a lot of time off. I could write, exercise, read and use the phone during the day. I would work in the late afternoon. The commissary guards treated you like a human. For prison, the commissary people were just straight fellas.

131

After a couple years I was camp eligible again. Duluth wanted nothing to do with me. So, a counselor gave me the old bait and switch. I saw it coming through the grapevine. I was transferred to Florence, Colorado Prison Camp. A bus ride, and a plane ride, and I was there. Located in central Colorado. The view from my room over looked Pikes Peak about 40 miles in the distance. This place was like a little Hamlet. The Camp was one of the four prisons on the same sprawling mountainside. The camp provided no security whatsoever. Two brick dormitories, and assorted brick buildings housing the everyday activities of the camp. We had no fences, or walls. We had wide-open mountainside.

Three other prisons were built on the mountainside. The FCI was well fenced in. The FCI was across the street. The Penitentiary was down the street, and the Ad Max, only had an entrance. This Maximum Security Prison was built into, and under the mountain. God only knows who is really in there. Without the razor wire, and walls, this area would look like a college campus.

June 21, 2000, I was released. A prison van left me off at the bus station in Florence. After eight and a half years, I stood alone, in front of the smallest bus station I had ever seen. After eight and a half years, one day a person says, "that's it Doctor. You are cured of bad doing. It's time to go," and off you go back into society. This was going to be a blast.

Two days of bus terminals, and junk food, I was smiling to see the Minneapolis skyline. Next stop was a halfway house on East Lake Street, in Minneapolis, for six months.

The halfway house was a converted mortuary. The halfway house rules were easy. A person, whom I have no desire to remember, instructed me that I needed a job of any kind. I had to pay twenty five percent of my gross pay to the halfway house. I needed to find my own transportation to and from work. The counselor smiled and asked, "That shouldn't be any problem for you after eight and a half years," he said laughingly. "No, as a matter of fact it will not be difficult," I responded grinning. "I could send you back to prison for six months, Doctor, just for insubordination," he said grinding his teeth. "Do what you got to do," I said.

So, the next morning my friend of forty years and his wife showed up at the halfway house. My pal Joe, and his wife Peggy, are the greatest people you could ever have the chance to meet. Joe and Peggy own the largest snow removal company in the Midwest, and a very successful poured wall foundation concrete company. The snow removal company covers part of the year. The concrete company goes strong in the summer months. But, the crews go year round pouring foundations.

Looking out the window of the halfway house lobby, I noticed Joe had driven his red convertible Mercedes. Peggy had driven a silver blue four door 300SD Mercedes. Joe and Peggy introduced themselves to my counselor. Other inmates in the lobby looked out into the morning sunshine, gleaming off the Mercedes cars.

Joe and Peggy explained how I would be working for their companies, and that they had given me the silver blue Mercedes for transportation. Joe pointed out the counselor's office window at the car. The counselor turned red, and redder.

In his outrage he wrote down the pertinent information. The counselor actually thought he could play a game of chess with the Doctor. I believe Gordon Liddy said it best to a Federal Warden. "This is a game of wits, and you sir, are unarmed."

So, life started in Minneapolis again. I sat in the Mercedes. I tuned the radio into Tom Barnard and the 92 KQRS radio morning show gang. I opened the sunroof, and listened to some excellent street humor from the morning show crew.

Prison wasn't good, and it wasn't bad. The main thing in this game is to realize that, sooner or later, prison is part of the game.

I'm presently writing A HEART FOR FAITH. This book tells of the trials of a seven-year-old girl in need of a heart transplant.

My other project is LAWFUL DECEIT. The true story of a man paying enormous child support fees, to a child who is not his. The law says he has to pay, until he can bring the real father to justice. The female with child only had to say it was his, because he just happened to be rich. Two governors' offices agree to help find the real father. DNA reveals the father. This does not end so quickly though.